EXTRA CREDIT

Jeff Black

EXTRA CREDIT

Boston · Alyson Publications, Inc.

This is a paperback original from Alyson Publications, Inc., PO Box 2783, Boston, Mass. 02208. Distributed in England by Gay Men's Press, PO Box 247, London, N15 6RW.

First edition, May, 1985   5 4 3 2 1

ISBN 0 932870 70 8

To Don Henderson:
with gratitude and affection
because I can't afford to pay you back in cash.

e were standing at the top of the stairs talking, bathed in the dim fluorescent light peculiar to schools of a certain era. Rose was doing most of the work. The exact meaning of her words failed to register in my mind, but the manner in which her thin eyebrows charged together above her nose to form a hairy bat just beginning its ominous swoop told me that whatever those words meant, they were meant passionately. I nodded or shook my head at what seemed the appropriate moments, and I was soon adept at anticipating the approach of yet another paragraph's triumphant climax. The words were merely an unrolling series of sound, a ribbon of noise winding its way through the air.

The chants echoing down the hall tumbled up toward us and severed that ribbon in mid-glottal stop: "Fight, fight, fight, fight."

"Oh god," I groaned. "Only second period and already..."

But Rose's attention was drawn to the growing disturbance in the corridor below. Always one for a challenge, she broke into a run. "Come on, Harper," she cried over her shoulder at me, her little heels clicking on the black and gray tile in a firm cadence. "You know what to do."

Well frankly, no I didn't. In five years of teaching, I had through stealth and cowardice avoided every fight that had occurred in my vicinity. At twenty-six, I felt with some conviction that I should do everything possible to insure my passage on to twenty-seven. Chester A. Arthur Junior High School was known area-wide as the facility requiring the most ambulance runs three years in a row. Despite the frequency of the fights, I always managed to avoid having to deal with them. Never had I been required to separate two thrashing teenagers lusting for blood. (They seldom cared whose blood was spilled.) Avoiding confrontation was not easy; my untarnished record should not be taken lightly. I ducked into the nearest classroom, slipped into the lounge, crouched behind a desk as if retrieving something, or just pivoted and strode briskly away. Screams and thuds may have assailed my ears, and dust may have risen around me, but I refused to acknowledge the existence of any scuffle, that word defined, in administrationese, as anything from a playful pat on the back of the head to a duel with pistols at dawn.

One of my most anxious moments came when I went into the boy's restroom in order to miss a three-person altercation taking place further down the hall. My relief abandoned me upon entering, for I discovered four boys shoving a less fortunate fifth into a toilet, head first. Their response to the sputtering boy's struggles was one of total glee. "Look at him splash!" one of them cried, "Look at that sucker splash!" Then they saw me. We stared across the restroom in silence. Their eyes showed anger and fright. One boy's eye was puffy and blue. The only sounds were the occasional aquatic thrashings of the thin figure disappearing into the plumbing. I stared at them, unsure of what to do. Then they dropped the boy and pushed past me roughly, escaping through the swinging door into the hall. The harassed one stood slowly, water streaming down his head and staining his light blue shirt navy. He was a frail boy, utterly humiliated as he stood before me. He retrieved his glasses and wiped his face. He looked at me unblinking, silent. I shook my head and whispered, "I'm sorry." Like a frightened animal, he too bolted from the restroom, leaving me to press my head against the cool beige tile.

Yet, here I was watching Rose's diminishing figure and knowing that I would follow her downstairs to the fight. I was totally unequipped to supervise educational mayhem but Rose McCormack, mighty chairperson of the English department, had commanded it and I must obey or face the consequences — and consequences were Rose's strong suit. I broke into a run.

"Fight, fight, fight, fight!"

Students poured into the hall from all directions, alerted by some form of communication spread telepathically throughout the sprawling school. This scuffle must be a major one. I was not thrilled. I passed several teachers as I hurried down the hall, all of them going in the opposite direction. I wasn't the only one who refused to bulldog the kids. "If God had wanted teachers to have guard duty," a grizzled biology teacher once said, "He wouldn't have created Dobermans."

I waved briefly at Connie Masters, peering cautiously out of her classroom. Her violently red hair was tied back with an outrageous purple scarf. She waved the tip of her ponytail at me. "Be brave little soldier," she said. I noticed the new teacher, Garrick Dobson, peeking from Connie's room as well. I stopped and blushed in greeting. He blushed back on cue. "Want to help?" I asked.

"Harper King!" Connie cried. "Give the poor child a break. It's only his second week for god's sake."

"I hate to miss the fun," Garrick added on his own behalf, "but I think I'll pass."

"Quite all right. Want a souvenir limb?"

"Sounds great."

"An arm or a leg?"

"Surprise me."

And I was off again.

The students at Chester A. Arthur cherished a good fight, most especially when injury was incurred. Blood, of course, was ideal. To prolong the sometimes titanic struggles, they formed a protective circle around the combatants, locking hands, thus making it difficult if not impossible for authorities to reach the bout. This peer conspiracy, symbolized by their joined hands, impressed me both as a statement of vulnerability and strength. And now I was expected to plow my way through their barrier. Rose and I stood at the perimeter of the shouting mass of kids. Their hands were locked, fingers firmly gripped around their neighbors' wrists. We were totally ignored. I can't say I was sorry. Catching my breath at least ten yards from the actual fight, I hoped their blockade worked forever. Rose, however, used to being treated with respect or a reasonable facsimile of the same, was trembling with frustration. She pushed and pulled and threatened the kids, but was unable to penetrate the defiant circle of students. As I sighed with relief, I thought I heard Rose growl.

I heard someone in front of me say that the fight was between two girls. I was secretly pleased. Girls' fights are usually the best. Boys only use their fists and constantly look at the crowd to see the reaction to their performance. But girls abandon themselves completely, fighting with their very souls while not forgetting the effectiveness of their nails. If you have to fight, the kamikaze spirit found in the girls seems essential.

A boy was hoisted up on a neighbor's shoulders from where he began giving a blow by blow description of the fracas below. "Maggie grabs Theresa by the hair and knocks her on the ground. Look at her head hit the floor. Maggie's pulled a handful of hair out Theresa's head. Anybody want a wig? Now she's on top of Theresa smacking her face. Wait! What a comeback! Theresa grabs her Lit book and grinds it into Maggie's forehead."

Rose was nearly hysterical with frustration. "We've got to do something, Harper!" she shouted. I shrugged noncommitally. I found myself attracted to the crowd of kids, now silent as they watched with intense fascination. (It was rather like the fascination one has while having great sex and not believing just how great it is, concentrating on it just to measure the depth of the feeling.) Stepping on my feet occasionally, backing into me with more regularity, they turned to apologize until they recognized me as a teacher. Then even those who liked me and would speak to me under normal circumstances gave me a dirty look. Fighting was basic in the school, and when it came to the basics, I was the enemy. But there was an excitement that connected me to these kids. A thin blue cord, it seemed, transferred their energy to me. What would they do if I clasped hands with them? Allow me to join their society? Or gladly break my hands?

Rose was still surveying the crowd for signs of a chink in its armor. I was rooting for Theresa, whoever she may turn out to be. Maggie was undoubtedly Maggie Swenson, a classroom bitch and a card-carrying tramp at age fourteen. Respected by her peers as a sexual *wunderkind*, she reportedly already had blow jobs in her repertoire. She had been in my class the year before, and more than once I had been tempted to take a swat at her myself.

The commentator, still on a tall buddy's shoulders, continued his broadcast of the melee, an invisible microphone in one hand, the other holding shaggy blonde hair out of his eyes.

"They're still rolling around, sports fans. Give 'em room, boys, give 'em room. Maggie scratches Theresa's cheek.

Blood! Theresa tries to scratch Maggie back but she doesn't have any fingernails. Let that be a lesson to you nailbiters. But Theresa is battling back again. She grabs Maggie's blouse and ... Hey man! Tit!"

The crowd surged forward, the protective barrier of locked hands suddenly disintegrating, once-idle spectators now clamoring for a glimpse of bare flesh. Rose saw her chance. She threw me in front of her and used my body as reluctant interference as she propelled us into the ogling crowd. We pushed past denim elbows and denim knees; we bumped into denim shoulders and denim asses. It was a descent into a hell designed by Levi Strauss. During the rough and tumble trip, I smelled cigarettes, pot, whiskey, baby powder, perspiration and Oil of Olay. It reminded me of a night at the bar. Suddenly we popped into the center of the surprised circle, where Maggie and Theresa were still busily tearing at one another. Maggie's hair was matted with blood, and her left breast jiggled intermittently into view. (Maggie and her avocado-sized gland were the sentimental favorites.) The other girl, Theresa, had five bloody skid marks down her pale face. Tufts of her hair lay at her feet. Rose and I were greeted with hisses and boos as we appeared. Rose was not intimidated by their response; for once I was glad of her bravado.

"All right!" she roared. "The fight is officially over. Everybody back to class. This is a school not Madison Square Garden. Move!"

At first no one budged and I expected to be fallen upon by a swarm of angry teenagers. I recognized most of them: some good kids, some not so good, most in between, some who were fighters themselves, others who would gasp at the very idea. Their collective face was a total blank. Then, like a flock of thin-legged birds soundlessly lifting off the surface of a reed-filled lake en masse, they turned and walked away without once glancing behind them. This too I felt deeply, another show of strength intertwined with an admission of weakness.

Rose took Maggie into custody with the delicacy of a prison matron. Theresa, I assumed, was to be my property. Unlike Maggie, she was not a pretty girl, and apparently did nothing to improve her looks. What was left of her hair was dirty and uncombed; her baggy, wrinkled clothing begged for attention. She slouched, head bowed, pallid face averted. I put my arm gently around her shoulder.

"Mr. King," Rose said.

"Mrs. McCormack?"

"Hold her arm so. Anything more comforting is not required. Arms around shoulders are for accident victims, the elderly and one's date to the junior prom. They are not for hoodlums such as these."

"She started it!" Maggie shouted. Rose and I both automatically placed our bodies between the two girls. I found myself close to Rose, uncomfortably close considering the emptiness now around us.

"What should we do with them now, Mr. King?" Rose asked in a tone I recognized from having observed her in her classroom: this was a quiz.

"Why Mrs. McCormack, have you forgotten? School regulations state that we must now take them directly to the principal's office."

"It's nice to know you're aware of the regulations. In all your years here, I don't believe I've ever seen you supervising a scuffle."

"I like to keep a low profile. Negotiate behind the scenes."

"She started it!" Maggie cried again.

"You keep quiet missy," Rose ordered.

"Bitch!" The word was spat out even as her lips realized what they were saying and tried to retrieve them. Rose bristled and she jerked Maggie across the hall, shoving her roughly up against the wall. Her words were too low to hear, but the tone, like distant thunder, was threatening. I walked Theresa to the other side of the corridor. She was about to cry.

"What happened?" I asked.

"Nothing."

"Nothing does not make a face bleed. Who started the fight?"

"She did. Well, me. I mean we both did. They were calling me ugly and I told them to shut up."

"Who said that?"

"Maggie and her friends."

Behind us Rose suggested that we proceed to Mr. Prynne's office in accordance with regulations. "Act nice in Prynne's office," I whispered to Theresa. "Don't argue with him. Let me do the talking." She wiped one eye dry with the back of her hand. She nodded again. Then, touching the scratches on her face, she winced and looked at the blood on her fingertips. "Ouch," she moaned.

Theresa and I walked over to Rose and Maggie, the latter momentarily cowed. We marched smartly down the hall until we passed Garrick Dobson's classroom. It appeared empty. Rose backtracked and peered into that part of the room obscured from my view.

"Are you free this period, Mr. Dobson?"

There was a silence.

"Is that a nod of assent?" she asked, indicating that vocal responses were necessary when dealing with her.

"Yes." Garrick did not sound pleased.

"Then come with me. Mr. King and I have just broken up a scuffle. You need to see what happens next in this process."

Garrick practically slithered from his room, rolling his eyes helplessly in my direction when Rose wasn't looking. It all seemed so foolish to me. So useless. And I knew that it was no way for a teacher to feel. What was wrong with me, I wondered?

Rose threw open the door to the Administrative Suite (principal's office) and announced that she wanted to see Mr. Prynne immediately. Her booming request cut short the amiable conversation of the school's secretaries, Mary and Regina. They blushed and attempted to appear busy. Mary, the gentle widow of a Nazarene minister, pretended to type. She was the last person to realize there was no paper in the machine. She stood slowly, forcing a smile, and moved to the marred counter separating her from an unhappy Rose.

"May I help you, Mrs. McCormack?" Mary asked. Her hair was in its usual crescent-roll hairdo, a number two pencil buried in the mound, a yellow missile downed on a protein-rich peak.

"The sounds of work are infinitely less noisy than the sounds of idle chatter," Rose intoned in that way of hers that made everything sound like a quotation from the Bible.

The other secretary, Regina, leaped from her desk, her periwinkle beads landing with a hollow thump on her breastbone. "I'll go see if Mr. Prynne can be disturbed," she panted, bumping into her desk before disappearing behind a far door. We were silent.

I stared out the window where the warm sunlight of an early September morning was preparing to become the hot sunlight of the same sort of September afternoon. A car pulled into the parking lot. A small boy carrying a trombone case emerged from it after one, two, three attempts. I wished he'd release the instrument from its case. I pictured the slide flashing and winking in the sun. I wanted nothing more than to be out in the nice weather, stretching and relaxing, with school far behind me. Rose had her head tilted as if listening to distant music, probably a dirge, I thought. Somewhere a pencil was savagely sharpened, perhaps in preparation for entry into Mary's coiffure. I wanted to see the sun rise over that hair of hers just once before I died.

"Oh, Mr. Dobson!" Mary cried, startling us all. I clutched my chest in feigned cardiac arrest and staggered backwards gasping. "I have a letter for you. The other Mr. Dobson, down in the Industrial Arts department, got it by mistake. It's postmarked Pittsburgh. I thought it might be important."

"I wish they'd get it straight," Garrick sighed. "I'm *Garrick* Dobson, not *Elmo* Dobson. Can't anyone tell the difference between a 21-year-old English teacher and a 61-year-old Industrial Arts teacher?"

"You're the one without the bandaids on his fingers," I answered.

"It's probably from my mother. She gets a kick out of writing me here. My son the teacher and all that."

Rose broke in. "Perhaps you should inform your mother that this is not a summer camp." She was trying to be funny. The left side of her face twitched momentarily, a sure sign of amusement.

Regina made her way back into the office. "Mrs. McCormack," she said reverently, "Mr. Prynne says he wants to see you about another matter first. Then he'll see the rest of you."

Rose told us to sit, then went to confer with Greg Prynne. With impressive dramatics, Regina put a limp wrist to her forehead and swayed precariously. "I can't take any more of this."

"Come with me," Mary said, pulling on Regina's arm. "Help me with the absence list. Don't worry about the phones. I've unplugged them." She heaved open the door and, half-supporting Regina, exited.

"I don't believe it." Garrick said.

"What?"

"Elmo Dobson opened my letter and read it."

"How do you know?"

"The envelope is open."

"Maybe Mary opened it."

"Mary doesn't usually have axle grease on her fingers."

"Good point."

While Garrick read his stained letter, I steered Theresa to an orange plastic chair and told her to sit. I pointed to a yellow chair across the room and told Maggie to sit as well.

"I don't have to," she sassed.

"You're right, Maggie."

"I am?"

"The only things you have to do are pay taxes and die."

"Huh?"

"And it isn't tax time, dear."

She sat, but not without signs of suspicion.

I looked around the office. The wallpaper was vinyl, an orangish color I'd never seen outside of slightly aged pumpkins. A pigeonhole mailbox mercifully covered one wall. Each teacher had his very own pigeon hole, barely big enough for an average envelope and certainly not capable of containing anything larger without permanent wrinkling. Another wall supported a nearly empty bulletin board. Three scraps of paper hung at jaunty angles from the pitted board: a sheet with rules apropos to fire, tornado and nuclear holocaust; an announcement concerning a faculty pitch-in dinner; and a thank-you note sent by Jean Taylor following the death of her husband nearly two years before.

"What happens next?" Theresa asked me.

"I'm not sure. Maybe detention."

"That's not what happens," Maggie snapped.

"Oh yes, I forgot. Maggie here is an expert at these proceedings. Is that the chair with your name engraved on it?"

"Real funny, Mr. King."

I sat beside Theresa and nudged her gently in the side. "You haven't had a lot to say," I whispered.

"You told me to be quiet."

"You okay?"

"What's going to happen?"

"I'm not sure. I've never done this before."

"What do you think might happen?"

"I guess we'll go into Mr. Prynne's office and talk about the fight."

"Then what?"

"Maybe we'll decide whose fault it was."

"And then?"

"Then? Well, then perhaps we'll talk about punishments."

"And then?"

"My God, Theresa. And then we'll call in the press so they can witness the executions. You got in a fight, you didn't sell government secrets to the enemy. Don't be so scared. I told you I'd take your side."

"But you don't understand," she moaned, putting her head in her hands. "If I get in trouble, I might be sent away."

"Away?"

"To Minnesota. That's where my mother lives."

"Your parents are divorced?"

"And I live with my father. I moved here this summer when my mother got married again. Dad doesn't like me living with him. He says I cause trouble."

"Then maybe you're better off with your mother."

"She doesn't want me either. Her new husband doesn't like me. And he has a daughter who's a cheerleader. Jesus. Sorry, Mr. King."

"I promise I'll do the best I can for you." I patted her on the shoulder, wondering about the quality of my best.

Rose reappeared long enough to grunt "Now" before marching back into the oblivion of Greg's office. First Theresa, then Garrick, Maggie and I loped across the room, showing a complete lack of enthusiasm for our destination.

Greg Prynne's office was the windowed but dark cubicle of a self-proclaimed man's man. A stuffed trout inhaled sadly as it looked down upon the desk of the man who had tempted it with a plastic dragonfly. There was a map of Southeast Asia on the wall left over from the days when Greg kept track of the war in Vietnam. On the desk was a framed photo of him shaking hands with a former vice-president. The vice-president's eyes were closed. Greg leaned over the desk and bestowed looks of grave dissatisfaction upon Maggie and Theresa, both seated before him. He was fifty but looked much younger. Trim and solid and undeniably attractive. His eyebrows were remarkable. Dark mobile things, they defied all known physical rules as they unrolled one at a time over a brown eye, like a hirsute venetian blind. "What do we have here?" he growled.

Rose supplied the answer.

"Fighting, eh, Mrs. McCormack?"

"Like two animals."

"Maggie I know, but who's this one?"

Rose eyed Theresa as if she were a hair in her tomato soup. "I've never seen her before."

"What's your name?"

Theresa hung her head and was silent.

"I said what's your name. Did Maggie beat you deaf?"

"Theresa."

"Louder."

"Theresa. My name is Theresa."

"Theresa what?" Rose asked, not missing a beat.

"Laugermann."

"Laugermann?"

Theresa nodded. Rose and Greg stood side by side facing the girls, their stances similar, backs rod-straight, hands across stomachs (hers had a slight paunch) and thumbs twiddling. Greg's right eyebrow did its trick, drooping momentarily over an eye before repositioning itself in his sour but craggily attractive countenance.

"What exactly were they doing?" he asked.

"When I arrived in the English hall they were rolling on the tile in an unbelievable fashion. Maggie was practically naked and this one, Theresa, was covered with blood. I broke it up immediately, of course. Then Maggie called me a name."

"A bitch," I offered in my most concerned of tones. Garrick swallowed a giggle. Rose looked at me a moment without speaking, then told Greg that I had been at the fight too.

"You, King?" Greg asked ironically.

"I played a very minor role."

"And where do you fit in, Dobson?"

"I'm an apprentice."

"I felt he needed to see how this process worked," Rose explained. "New teachers can't wait a semester or two to learn the ropes. It's all out there from day one."

"An exemplary idea, as usual, Mrs. McCormack."

"What about us?" Maggie asked, rising. "Can we go now?"

"Stay in your seat. Okay, girls, who started this?"

"She did!" Maggie cried, pointing at Theresa.

"What do you have to say about that, Theresa?"

"No."

"What?" Greg commanded. "Louder."

"I didn't start it."

"Then who did?"

"Maggie did."

"Did not!" came Maggie's scream. "Liar!"

A pleading look from Theresa told me that if I was to come to her defense, I'd better do it soon. Greg and Rose were completing their final circling before moving in for the kill. I was surprised at how strongly I agreed with Theresa's position. She had every reason to fight. Maggie had tormented her and it was her duty to slug her. In theory, I would have decked her too. In fact, I probably would have just taken the abuse quietly, as I had on several occasions in my life. But I wanted to help Theresa get away with it.

I cleared my throat. "I've been talking to Theresa outside and she told me that Maggie and her friends were calling her names. She asked them to stop and they wouldn't. That's when the fight started."

"But who started it?" Rose asked.

"Maggie did," I replied. "When she called Theresa names."

"Sticks and stones," Rose clucked. "Sticks and stones."

Greg pointed a finger at Theresa. "What about it? She call you names?"

"Yes."

"What names?"

"Just names."

"What names were they calling you?"

"Ugly."

"Louder."

"Ugly. Maggie called me ugly."

"But who started the fight?" Rose chimed in.

"Maggie," I repeated between clenched teeth; I was more than a little angry at their blindness. "She started it when she called Theresa ugly. It's no wonder Theresa fought back."

"But she still fought," Rose pointed out.

I tried to explain the difference between fighting and fighting back, but Greg would not listen. He asked me why I was being so difficult. An eyebrow drooped again, this time at me.

"I don't mean to be difficult, Gr— . . . Mr. Prynne. I happen to think there is a clear difference in the ways in which Theresa and Maggie acted."

"Nevertheless," he sighed, "Both girls were found—"

"May I say something?" Garrick asked from near the door,

where he had been recently ignored.

"Dobson?"

"Are you confused about something?" Rose wanted to know. "I'll explain everything later."

"I'm not confused. There's just something I want to say that might help you clear this thing up."

Greg told him to proceed.

"I have both Theresa and Maggie in my second period class. They had their fight just after they left me. Today I had to get after Maggie three times to stop teasing Theresa."

"Did not," Maggie sneered. I put a firm hand on her shoulder and, recoiling, she grew silent.

Garrick continued. "Maggie threw little bits of eraser at Theresa. She kicked her books down the aisle. She called her stupid and made fun of her clothes. And I distinctly heard her say Theresa was ugly."

"Has this been going on since school started?" I asked, and Theresa nodded. "I don't see how we can expect anyone to be teased like this and not want to fight back. Theresa knows that fighting in school is not good. She knows she's in trouble. But shouldn't we understand that she felt she had to fight after being tormented like that?" My voice stopped on a quavering note of passionate anger. More than a student fight was affecting me.

Rose shook her head. "They were fighting in school. Period. That's that."

"I agree, Mrs. McCormack," Greg said. "Both of you are suspended for three days. Thank you, Mrs. McCormack. Dobson. King. You may go. You girls stay parked. We're going to have a little talk."

Theresa's head dangled sadly; her chin lay on her chest. Just as well; if she'd been looking at me, I couldn't have met her eye. Rose nudged Garrick and me into the outer office. She turned on me immediately.

"Harper King, I cannot emphasize too strongly how much I disapprove of teachers pleading a student's case, especially in front of that student. It is unwise. It is irresponsible. I assume you'll take my advice."

I didn't answer. For once, she took my silence as assent.

"And you Garrick. I've taught in this school for over twenty years. I know how things work. On a ship, what you two have just done would be considered mutiny. Luckily, Gregory Prynne is guiding our course, and he knows what to do with misplaced humanism. Now excuse me. My grandson's birthday is this weekend and I must finish knitting his sweater."

She pushed her way through the door. Garrick finally got angry. "Theresa shouldn't be suspended," he cried, pounding a fist into the palm of his other hand.

"I think we tried to say that in there."

"Are they mad at us now?" he asked as we left the office.

"Not mad exactly. But they won't forget. They never forget. What are you doing tonight?"

"Nothing that I know of."

"No Friday night date?"

"No Friday night date. Why?"

"Connie's coming over to my house for drinks. We might go out later. I thought you might like to join us."

"Sure. Thanks."

"About eight-thirty would be good. I'll give you directions later."

As we neared the English corridor, the shouts rang out: "Fight, fight, fight, fight."

"Coffee?" I asked.

"I'm buying."

We turned on our heels and hurried to the lounge.

rzlp didl uwst nerp."

Connie Masters' voice came to me from the study at the back of my apartment where I had left her leaning against the wall, smoking a cigarette and trying to perfect her fire-breathing dragon imitation.

"What?" I called from the kitchen at the opposite end of my labyrinthine apartment.

"Vrzlp didl uwst nerp."

I shrugged and continued making myself a drink, holding an ice cube up to the light. I am one of the few people I've heard of who finds some personal aesthetic need satisfied by the sight of tiny bubbles suspended in an ice cube. That night I was drinking scotch and soda, not my favorite drink, but not unpleasant if consumed in vast enough quantities. My natural alcoholic sympathies were torn between white wine and any-thing that required a paper umbrella, but I liked to experiment with different drinks. There is something to be said for variety in one's hangovers.

Connie and I were re-enacting what had become ritual over the last several years: meeting at her apartment or mine to drink, relax and talk. It was a comfortable ritual for the most part, although sometimes I thought that we would perform it out of sheer habit even if we did not consciously wish to. There were times when I longed to break the routine, but it was too ingrained to change without exhausting myself emotionally and alienating Connie. And in many ways we depended on these sessions for our psychic livelihoods. Sheltered away from school and the kids and all the sundry grotesqueries of life that seemed constantly to dog our heels, we recovered as best we could from the world. We chatted, we disagreed, we confessed, we confided, we accused. We healed ourselves and each other as best we could; we bound bleeding wounds temporarily while waiting for a permanent cure. Although neither of us told the other everything we thought and felt (secrets were our true best friends; keeping something in reserve is basic to being human) we knew more about the other's feelings and thoughts than anyone else in the world. Some might say that Connie and I knew too much about one another; that we left ourselves open and vulnerable should one or the other of us decide to turn nasty. But that was the price we were willing to pay for the opportunity to walk into a room together and shut out the world.

Our variegated encounters were most enjoyable, as a rule, when they took place in my study, actually a spare bedroom in the maze of my apartment. It was in this room that I did most of my real living. During my five years of residence there, I'd decorated the room according to my long-time ideal of what a study should be, a combination of dreams borne of a relatively book-free childhood (odd since I came from a family of educators) and four years of study in a sterile university library. I wanted a cozy place where I could read in peace, a room able to transport me into my reveries as nimbly as the books it housed. The hardwood floors had been rescued from wall-to-wall carpeting and subject only to a faded but proud throw rug at the far end of the long rectangular room. There was a fireplace at that end, now standing dark and lonely, preparing to belch smoke into my life and home come winter. On the mantel was the bust of an unidentified German gent I'd discovered at a garage sale, a bust consistently identified as Beethoven for some reason. To counteract the bust's puff-cheeked Germanic scowl I'd strapped a bright red bow tie around his neck. Three walls of the room were covered by bookshelves, and the fourth wall contained a television, stereo and hundreds of albums, though I played only a dozen of them regularly. Because they reminded me of school, I allowed no overhead lights in the room. In the corner by the aquarium, the Statue of Liberty with a barometer in her belly (the poor dear lady had begged me with tears in her amber eyes to help her escape from an antique show) softly illuminated the room with her shaded torch. Facing one another in the center of the room and separated by a long, low table, were a burgundy sofa and, opposite, a rocking chair and leather easy chair with matching hassock.

Connie was now stretched out on the sofa, her feet propped on one of its arms. As I entered the room, she lit another cigarette from the dying butt of the one dangling from her lips. She was constantly smoking, and the husky manner in which she said, "The return of the native," was not at all harmed by the unceasing procession of cigarettes. "If you see me without a cigarette," she'd once told me, "I'm either teaching, sleeping or dead. And those are all about the same thing in my book." She'd even admitted that during sex itself she'd often enjoyed a smoke or two. "You just have to be sure not to blow smoke in his face or to singe his ass. That last one really tends to kill the moment."

I plopped down in the leather chair across from Connie. "Did you say something a minute ago?" I asked, sipping my drink. "I couldn't hear you."

"I said there's been a tragedy. You'd better sit down, Harper."

"I am sitting down. Witness the bent waist and knees."

"So you are." She sighed. "There's been a death."

"A death?"

"Someone very close to you." She crushed out her cigarette in the ash tray and ran her fingers through her bright red hair. Her hair was thick and spirited, impossible to confine in any particular style. She'd long ago decided to let it run its course. Springing from her head as if alive and panicked, great shocks of it grew out to the sides and poured down her back. It was a crimson web, which, if translated into an emotion, would most certainly be surprise. Like her hair, Connie had a spontaneity and a refusal to be tamed that I admired but by which I felt a little cowed. Yet, while her hair seemed to thrive with its total freedom, Connie on the other hand was at times less than happy with her independence.

"Who died?" I asked.

"I don't know for sure. It's up to you to identify the body. Over in the aquarium. One of your fish passed on."

"A fish? Jesus, it's getting to be like Guyana in that tank. Maybe I should just have a fish fry and get rid of the damned things."

"I thought this would affect you more deeply."

"Fish owners get hardened to death." I crossed to the aquarium and looked into the murky violet water. An angel fish dipped and bobbed on its back. "It's the third one this week. You think I'm doing something wrong?"

Connie stood by my side. She too peered into the tank, flipping the ashes from her cigarette into the water. "Maybe you should get a cat," she said. "They're a lot harder to kill."

"These fish are defective."

"Count on Harper King to get fish with a death wish. Aren't you going to dispose of the body?"

Repositioned in my chair, I watched Connie as she perused the bookshelves. It mattered not that she'd done the same thing hundreds of times before, she now scoured them as if for the first time. It was all part of the ritual. Soon she would begin to tell me her woes. So I waited and watched.

Tonight she'd attempted to cover her hair with an orange scarf, one in a seemingly endless line of loud and tasteless accessories she insisted on placing in, over, or on her coiffure. The scarf matched her blouse, a minor fashion coup. Outfits that "matched" were boring she said. She liked the excitement of an outfit that clashed in just the right way, though she was hard pressed to describe exactly what this way might be. Her jeans were a deep stiff blue, and too tight. Inspired by my rather dramatic shedding of twenty-five pounds over the recently concluded summer vacation, she'd begun a serious weight-reducing regime after a few false starts. Recently, depressed by her slow progress, as an incentive she'd purchased several pair of pants in a smaller size. It seemed that she'd become impatient and had decided to pack herself into the still too-small jeans. Unfortunately, dieting would never solve all of Connie's shape problems. By nature she was oddly built. Petite north of her midriff, she was positively bulbous south of the equator. Her hips and thighs and ass swelled and swelled, like the products of a glassblower gone berserk, before her body returned to debutante size around her knees much too late and much to Connie's chagrin. "For centuries plump women have been adored," she'd once moaned. "I had to be born in the one era when anorexia is in."

Her structure did not give her an overall unattractive appearance, however. On the contrary, she had the safe, tried and tested attractiveness large women often have. There is a certain charm in a lack of subtlety — be it physical subtlety or otherwise — and Connie had it. She looked comfortable and many men, at least temporarily, had found it irresistible.

She left the books and paced aimlessly around the room. I could tell that there was something on her mind, that something was wrong. Her face changed according to the current condition of her mood: when happy, its permanently pink cheeks were smooth and unlined, but when disturbed, wrinkles and creases crept in, and she looked all of her forty years and more. As she wandered about my study, she looked tired. Lines appeared on her brow and around her mouth, her skin looked almost gray. The twinkle was absent from her blue eyes. And, instead of its usual semi-gentleness, her smile was thin-lipped and grim. She moved slowly around the room, stopping to put on an album, a bluesy torch singer defeated but trying to be brave. Another bad sign.

"What's wrong?" I asked.

"Nothing's wrong," she snapped too quickly. "Why should anything be wrong?"

Perhaps because she saved her complaints against life to dump on me during our weekly visits; but I said nothing. Whatever her mood, I hoped she got over it before Garrick Dobson arrived. He was to be there in less than an hour and I didn't want him walking in on a gloomy gathering. From him I detected the scent of possibility, though I couldn't be more specific than that. I was even a little nervous about his arrival, rather like a school girl awaiting her first date. Silly me, I thought. And beyond any personal reasons I might have for wanting to show him a good time, humanitarianism dictated that he enjoy himself. God knows he probably wasn't getting much enjoyment out of teaching at Arthur.

I tried again. "Anything you want to talk about, Connie."

"Get off my back god damn it. I said there wasn't anything wrong. Leave me alone, will you?"

"And every time you say there's nothing wrong, you prove there is. You're going to tell me sooner or later. So make it sooner, will you?"

"How do you know I'll tell you?"

"You always do. So let's talk. Don't you want to get it out of your system before Garrick gets here?"

"So that's it. You don't care about me and my troubles. You just want to impress that child Garrick out of his pants and into who knows what orifice. Well, fuck you." With that, she stomped out of the study, her red hair waving like tatters behind her.

I was not especially concerned by this display of temper. Connie exploded with a frequency equalled only by Old Faithful, without the nuisance of littering tourists hanging about of course. She had achieved a certain notoriety among her acquaintances (one could not say she had any friends besides me) for possessing a marked lack of room in her personality for life's little irritations. The big problems, the disasters, she could cope with because she'd had so much experience with them: she was disaster's common-law wife. The smaller things destroyed her. I'd seen her depression and her fury, having to cope with the former and survive the latter when it was directed, as it often was, at me. It was in her nature to release her displeasure in brief but deadly spurts, as a boiler releases an excess and potentially dangerous build-up of steam. And it was in my nature to take what she dished out, for to try to change it would take too much energy, and I saw no reason to expend the energy, especially when I had nothing better to take the place of her friendship.

I took Connie's absence from the study as an opportunity to dispose of my deceased fish. I met her in the hall on my way to the bathroom. "Where are you going?" she asked quite amiably, as if her emotional outburst had never occurred.

"Don't you see the little flag on my antennae? This is a funeral procession."

"Poor little fishie." She petted the corpse in my hand. "Did it have a name?"

"Richard the Second."

"You name your fish after the kings of England?"

"Of course not."

"After Shakespearian characters? Famous homosexuals?"

"Haven't I ever told you? One of my secrets about to be revealed. I name them after my old lovers. I've slept with two men named Richard. Thus, Richard the Second. At one time, before they started their belly-up numbers, all the emotional and sexual involvements of my life were represented in that fish tank."

"I thought it was a little crowded in there."

"Oddly enough, they seem be dying in the order that I went to bed with the originals."

"How strange. Will you let me flush?"

"Be my guest."

Proper rituals were followed. Chants were spoken into the porcelain bowl. Connie reached for the handle while I tore paper into small bits and sprinkled it over the body. The toilet was flushed and Richard the Second disappeared from view as quickly as the inspiration for his name had disappeared from my life.

We returned to the study where we set up the back-gammon board. Connie lay on her stomach on the sofa and I sat on the floor. The board lay between us on the table. As the game began, I asked her again what was bothering her. This time she was willing to talk.

The consuming despair of her life was the continuing bad luck she experienced in her love life. From a fiance killed in Korea, to a disastrous three-year marriage she'd rebounded into while mourning her soldier, to a string of affairs that collapsed under their own absurdly writhing weight, Connie's emotional life was one three-alarm fire after another from which there rarely escaped any survivors. Although she described the situation in her patented mock-heroic style, they were a source of real and constant pain to her. I knew better than anyone how bitter her experiences with men had made her, and how stunted and gnarled her heart had become. Yet still she expected to stumble across a perfect love, and I did little to talk her out of this belief, for in my own way I was looking for the same thing.

"It's been four months since I've had a date," she said, lazily moving a backgammon tile.

"With your track record, isn't that a blessing?" I wasn't being cruel. I knew from experience that the quickest way to restore her spirits was to tease her.

"It isn't right for someone my age to go without a man."

"It isn't right for someone any age," I replied, thinking more of myself than of her, fourteen years older than me but not more hopeful of a successful relationship. I kept my hopes to myself, however.

"I have a lot to give to a man," Connie insisted.

"And you have dozens of happy customers to back up the claim."

"I'm serious, Harper. I'm going through withdrawal. I'm not getting my government recommended daily dosage of required sexual attention. Masturbation is fine for awhile, but come on, it gets old. I made a date with my vibrator the other night, and even it stood me up."

"I get two stories from you," I cried. "When you're dating someone you complain that if you ever get to be independent again you'll slaughter a lamb to the god of isolation. But when you get out from under it all, you bitch and moan and can't wait until the whole crazy cycle starts again. You can't have it both ways, girl."

"I know there are contradictions. I'm not blind. But that doesn't mean I don't feel all of this. It makes it all the worse. Maybe I should go back into therapy."

I reminded her that she said that therapy had done her no

good. She'd even told me once that weekend sessions with me had done her more good than two years with a woman who believed screaming and rolling about on the floor was the surest path to psychic stability. All she'd gotten out of those two years were exorbitant bills and floor burns.

Connie took her dice and rubbed them absently on her cheek, sighing. "I can forget how I feel most of the time. It takes some effort but I can forget. But sometimes it all comes crashing in on me. I walk around my apartment looking for some sign of a man who loves me. A discarded beer can, a jock thrown in the corner. Something. Anything. It's hard to take sometimes, you know?"

"I know." And I did. My search for a perfect lover was not quite her quixotic journey but it was painful enough thank you. Connie's articulation of her loneliness only underscored my own. I tried to change the subject. "What kind of music should we play when Garrick gets here? What kind do you think he likes?"

But Connie wanted to change the subject to something more of her liking. "What's it like being gay?"

"We've talked about this a hundred times. Let's not go through it tonight."

"Tell me. What's it like?"

"Being gay is a lot like *Where the Boys Are* without Connie Francis. Okay?"

"No really. Describe it to me."

"By knowing me, you can get a pretty good idea of what it's like. At least what my kind of being gay is like."

"Why are you gay?"

"Why all the questions? Have you decided to give it a go with women? You have my permission." I got up and put on another record, this time dance music, something upbeat.

"On the way over here I tried to make up a list of what I wanted in a man. I came up with a pretty fair description of you. Except you're gay. How come? I want to know why to-night you might be sleeping with a boy named Garrick rather than a woman like me."

"Tits have always confused me. And who says I might sleep with Garrick? Do you know something? He isn't even gay. Is he?"

"Don't ask me. You're the expert in that department. I assumed he was, the way you salivate around him."

"I do not salivate over Garrick Dobson. You talk about him as if he were a plate of stroganoff. Did I tell you I got a new pair of head phones?" I promptly plugged them in and fastened them to my ears, terminating our conversation. I was embarrassed and angry at Connie for recognizing my interest in Garrick, and angry at myself for not hiding that interest from her better. I knew how she could be when I had my hopes up over a man. I was in control of myself around Garrick (control in my case was a by-product of emotional sloth), and I did not wish to have him love me or to bear my child, but I did feel the potential for something special to happen between him and me. There was something about him, an easiness, a straightforward manner, that touched me deeply and set off my alarms.

Connie pulled the head phones from my ears. "Someone's knocking at the door," she said.

"Probably Garrick."

"The moment of truth is upon you my son."

"Shut up. Do I look all right?"

"Like one of Pavlov's dogs. Wipe the drool from your chin."

"I said shut up."

"Fuck you, Harper. You never did tell me why you're gay."

"My mother was frightened by a decorator when she was carrying me. Satisfied?"

"Not in years."

We went to the door and found Garrick lying face up in the hall, his arms and legs akimbo. He still had on his school clothes. Though he tried to pretend he was unconscious, the effort was in vain. He shook with giggles as the light from my apartment fell on his prone and provocative figure.

"Mail's here," Connie called.

"I've told them to slip it under the door," I replied, thinking more of male than mail.

"I can't take any more!" Garrick announced from the floor. "What a horrible, horrible day!" Connie and I pulled him to his feet and led him inside the apartment. "Is that a drink?" he asked. "Oh, I want a drink. Make it a big one. And a strong one, too, please."

"Make mine big and strong, too," Connie said. "Except make mine a man."

I took Garrick's order and hurried to fill it while Connie took him into the study. I handed him his drink where he sat on the floor leaning against a large pile of pillows, like a pasha awaiting who knows what kind of service. He grabbed the glass and took three deep gulps.

"My neighbor is a nurse," I said. "Maybe I could go borrow an IV and strap you to the vodka bottle."

Connie asked him what had happened, but he waved a hand in her direction. "Let me rest a minute. I've only been working in the real world for two weeks now. This is my first totally rotten day. Being a responsible adult isn't what it's cracked up to be."

"It gets a lot better PR than it deserves," I agreed.

He took another large gulp of his drink and sat back more deeply into the multi-colored pillows. His looks were angelic, though masculine, soft and fair, more like a teenager than an adult. His was a nearly cliché sort of good looks: blue eyes, white blond hair, enviable teeth, a combination that did not usually cross my threshold. Connie didn't find him at all attractive. "If you like that sort of thing, I suppose he's all right," she'd snorted. "He seems a little overdone to me. He'd be right at home in *Death in Venice*." The only odd bit of his anatomy that I could see (and I of course had not been privy to all of it), was the placement of his eyes. They were too close together for my taste, though it did not make him in the least unattractive. Their placement only intensified his gaze. He looked at me as if he'd blocked out all the world, focusing just on me. His apparent close scrutiny of me made me feel as if I were being pinned against a wall, not an unpleasant feeling when it was someone like Garrick doing the pinning.

"Do you know where I've spent my evening?" he finally asked, pointing an electric blue pillow first at me, then Connie. He did not wait for us to guess. "Yours truly has just spent three hours with Mrs. McCormack and her husband."

"With Rose?" I cried. "Oh god. If I'd known that I'd have made your drink stronger."

"I had dinner with them." He smiled, revealing his obscenely straight, white teeth. He had one of those flexible, almost rubbery smiles. When he got tickled by something he'd break into a wide Huck Finn, gee-shucks grin.

"You what?" Connie asked in disbelief.

"I had dinner with Rose McCormack and her husband Peter. Harper, do you remember how Mrs. McCormack walked past us in the parking lot after school while you were giving me directions here? After you drove off, she called me over to her car. She asked me how teaching was going and I said okay. She said we'd have to get together and talk over things every rookie should know and I said okay. What was I supposed to say? No, I don't want to talk to you and don't call me a rookie? She apologized for not spending more time with me but she'd been real busy and I said that's okay don't worry about it. I don't want to know what every rookie should know.

She kept asking me questions all the time she was changing her shoes."

"Her shoes?" Connie echoed.

"She has a special pair of driving shoes. She gave me some involved reason that went on and on. I tuned it out. It was about reaction time and swollen ankles. Then she said she'd heard you and me talking, Harper, and wondered if we were making plans for the evening and I said yes and she frowned and I asked her if there was something wrong."

"And," I interrupted, "She said there were several things wrong with you fraternizing with me, not the least of which is that I'm not a team player."

"Something like that. She called you an iconoclast and she shuddered when she said it like it was another word for leper. She said your priorities were confused and that I should try not to adopt your attitudes. Oh. Maybe I shouldn't be telling you this."

"She's told me the same things many times before. And I'll be hearing it a lot more. I'm up for tenure this year and Rose will have a big say in whether or not I get it. Did she mention our little confrontation in Greg Prynne's office this morning?"

"Not directly. But she implied the hell out of it. Don't worry. I told her that I like you and she said yes yes I like Harper too but he isn't the type of person you need to be close to while trying establish yourself as a teacher."

"Harper has never been Rose's favorite," Connie laughed.

"She told me to stay away from you too, Connie."

"What?"

"Same reasons?" I asked.

"Not so much that as the fact that Connie is a woman alone and I shouldn't get myself tangled up with women alone especially at my age because it could jeopardize my role as a teacher. I said I like you too and she said yes yes I like Connie too but she said that you had a reputation as sort of. . ."

"Yes?"

"A seductress."

He waited for our laughter to subside before he continued the tale of his evening. Saying goodbye to Rose, he'd gone to his car. She returned to the building to retrieve her driving gloves (grip and protection were listed as reasons for these). Garrick's car wouldn't start. He tried and tried, keys jangling, his desperate attempts to start the car becoming more frantic as Rose, re-emerging from the school, approached him and tapped on the window. She nearly dragged him from the front seat so anxious was she to be of service. Keeping him from calling a tow truck, she insisted that he have dinner at her house. They could call a tow truck from there, she added. After a brief tour of her immaculate, knick-knack laden abode, Rose prepared a heavy but delicious meal while Garrick was offered various unwanted sections of the newspaper by her stoic husband, Peter. Over dinner, she'd launched into lengthy dissertations concerning education, life and power.

"It was so boring," Garrick cried, squeezing my knee for emphasis. (Connie coughed knowingly, but I ignored her.) "We talked discipline and basics and study hall procedures."

"Rose's greatest hits," I said.

"Sparkling dinner conversation. I finally just spaced her out. I hope my eyes weren't glazed over. Her husband didn't listen to her either. I think I saw him mumbling to his salad."

After dinner, with a few parting warnings about my character, a tow truck had finally been alerted. It fished the car from the school parking lot and carried it away to a garage. Still offering sound educational advice and libels against poor me, Rose had delivered him to my door. Garrick shuddered and asked for another drink.

When our conversation switched to Garrick and his life

and background, he suddenly became tentative with his answers. I'm a sucker for shyness, so I was thoroughly charmed by his reticence. Connie, however, kept pumping away with questions until he finally told us about himself. He was twenty-one years old and until he'd left for college had spent all his life in Pittsburgh. He was engaged at eighteen, broke it off at nineteen, lost his father in a car accident at twenty, and had not yet suffered the tragedy of his twenty-first year. He hoped the three-year jinx was over, but working at Arthur Junior did not bode well for its end.

For years he had wanted to be an architect, spending hours as a child drawing floor plans for houses he then had fantasies about living in. By the time he had enrolled in college, the passion for architecture had waned and he set his sights on law school. He was told that an English degree was as good as any in preparation for law school, so he gritted his teeth and wandered into the department. By his senior year, however, he was beginning to tire of going to school. The prospect of several more years of studying didn't appeal to him at all. Then his father died and the decision was made for him. Money stopped flowing and he was forced to look around for what he was best prepared to do in the world outside of college. His English degree became a liability. Because they were notoriously easy credits he'd taken some education classes, and a little vocational counseling told him that the thing he was nearest to being was an English teacher. Garrick hadn't been particularly enthused, but he needed a career in a hurry. His college placement office had done the rest, finding him a job in a field that wasn't supposed to have any jobs open. So, although his family in Pittsburgh was less than happy that he would be living two states away, Garrick found himself teaching junior high school in the Midwest.

"I sort of became a teacher on the spur of the moment," he said apologetically.

"You can always go back to law school later, can't you?" I asked.

"That's what I've been thinking lately. Most people in law school are older than twenty-one so it must not be too weird to wait before going. Maybe I'll teach a couple of years and maybe save more money and by then I'll know if I want to be a lawyer for sure. Right now I think I'd enjoy being independently wealthy. I'm not sure I'm cut out to be a teacher."

Connie, always one for seizing on news of a broken romance, asked Garrick why he hadn't gotten married. I felt a little disappointed that he apparently had interest in such things as betrothals. Garrick's response to her tactlessness was slow and thoughtful.

"We... I had been changing for a long time and I guess I should have known better than to plan it in the first place. We got engaged just before we graduated from high school. It seemed like the only thing to do at the time. The prom pictures turned out nice, so we figured the wedding pictures would be even better. Then I went to college and the last thing I wanted to do was get married. We fought all the time. On the phone, through the mail. It was awful. She wanted me to come home to Pittsburgh and get a job or at the very least go to school there. But I liked being away. No one knew what I was up to, you know? By Thanksgiving break I knew there was no way I could marry anyone. By Christmas I'd worked up the nerve to break up with her. Last summer she married my younger brother. A real comfortable situation at family reunions."

"Eighteen is a miserable time to get married," Connie said. "I was eighteen when I did and by the time I was your age I was divorced. You did the right thing by getting out of it."

Garrick asked me if I'd ever been married. Connie snorted and I blushed. "Only to my work," I answered, but the joke didn't work. Then it was time for my autobiography, and I treated Garrick to a more honest version than the standard one I usually gave new acquaintances.

I was born in Baton Rouge, but my family moved north to Springfield, Illinois, when I was still an infant. By the time reproduction ground to a halt, there were five King kids bounding about. I had landed directly in the middle of the throng. My father was a teacher, principal, and, finally, an assistant to the director of the office of education for the state. My mother was a housewife, an occupation that barely exists in its purest form any longer but was epidemic during my childhood. Mom was always working, it seemed, usually doing something someone else should have done earlier. My standard memory of her shows her bent at the waist, apron dangling, head inserted in the dryer as she played tug of war with a stubborn bit of underwear. I remember Dad mostly as a weary man in an easy chair, his legs stretched out before him, his tie loosened and his shoes off, a big toe popping out through a hole in one sock. With five kids to support, Dad's life was one long sigh.

Looking back, I see that my family was remarkably middle-class, remarkably average. Besides my family's size (and my later preference for finding men between my sheets, a fact I didn't reveal to Garrick in my bio) the only off-key note in our suburban symphony was our choice of employment. We all became teachers. Every one of us. At one point, before retirement and death thinned out the ranks a bit, there were seventeen teachers in the family. Education was without question the family business. We were never pressured, never persuaded, never subjected to recruiting speeches; we did it as if genetically programmed. As a male born into a samurai family becomes a samurai, a child born into the King clan became a teacher. I had no consuming desire to go through life with chalkdust on my trousers, but when it came time to choose my career, I chose teaching without a thought.

Garrick was astounded by the educational dynasty from

which I had been issued. A family of dentists, sure, he said, a family of lawyers, even a family of criminals, but a family of teachers? He thought there was something a little sick about that.

"School talk was part of growing up,," I explained. "For years I thought everyone talked about faculty meetings, Iowa reading scores and bulletin board concepts over dinner."

I asked Garrick what he thought of his first two weeks of teaching. He looked at the floor, mildly embarrassed. "I've discovered one thing about teaching I never expected or maybe it's something about myself. It turns out I'm sort of afraid of the kids."

"You'll get used to it," I replied. "Connie and I did."

"You mean you got over it?"

"No. You won't get over it. You just get used to being scared."

"They scare you too?" he asked.

"I think most everyone is scared in his own way. A lot of people won't admit it, of course. You just learn not to pay much attention to it. If you work around loud machinery you learn not to hear it after awhile."

Connie said that even a quick movement in her peripheral vision made her panic for a second. "Scares the hell out me. Part of the territory, I guess."

I went to the kitchen to make more drinks. I thought back to my first year of teaching. I'd realized very soon that the only career I had ever considered was something I was good at but something I just did not like. The family business suffocated me, though I had grown used to not breathing. It wasn't something that I'd admit to Garrick; it was hard enough admitting it to myself.

When I returned to the study carrying a tray with drinks and snacks (the latter were for Connie; I abstained now that I was sleek), Connie cried, "Guess what? You two are birds of a feather flocking together."

The look on Garrick's face, confused and embarrassed, told me something odd had happened in my absence. "Care to translate?" I asked.

"While you were gone, I told Garrick you were gay. And he said. . . You tell him what you said, child."

He hesitated. "I said I was gay too." He waited while I put the tray on the table for my reaction. Connie leaned forward to get a good look at it too. So I gave them none. I smiled at Garrick. "So you're gay too. Want a cracker?"

"That's it?" Connie asked.

"Of course not," I said apologetically. "Would you like some cheese with that?"

"I mean about being gay."

I destroyed a cracker and sifted the crumbs into her outstretched hand. "We'll talk about it some other time."

"Why not now?" she demanded.

"We wouldn't want to bore you. You'd be the odd man out, so to speak." I winked at Garrick conspiratorially. He smiled and the tension passed from his face.

For the next hour we spoke of many things, though Connie time after time tried to steer the conversation to the sexuality Garrick and I shared. In tandem, we steered it right back. I grew angry with her, because of her presumption and her apparent attitude toward Garrick. She dismissed anything he had to say with a bored flick of her hand, and ignored all of the dirty looks I lobbed in her direction. Garrick did not seem to register her condescension, chattering away, telling tales of his first two weeks of teaching.

She left the room momentarily and I apologized for her. "You'll have to forgive Connie. She'll be quite acceptable once she evolves."

·43·

"What are you talking about?" His loose-lipped grin spread across his face.

"Nothing. I do want to talk about being gay some time. If you want to, that is."

"I want to. There aren't a lot of people to talk to about it."

We were silent a moment as a feeling of intimacy swept over us. "Maybe I shouldn't ask," I asked anyway. "But is this why you broke up with your fiancée?"

"It's a pretty good reason, don't you think?"

I nodded as Connie re-entered the room. "Am I breaking up girl talk? Just kidding. Your sort is so sensitive. But you make great quiche. Who wants to go to Pay Days?"

Garrick asked if that was the big bar downtown. "Of course it is," Connie snapped. "What a child. But a pretty one, don't you think, Harper?"

I ignored her and asked if he wanted to go. He eagerly said that he did. We organized ourselves and plunged out of the apartment.

"Garrick," Connie said, as he headed for my car, "You simply must ride with me. Physical attack and all that. Harper, why don't you drive too? Who knows? This might be the night you finally get lucky. Wouldn't it be a shame to be without a car?"

Connie and Garrick pulled out ahead of me. So furious was I with Connie that I accidently threw my car into reverse and demolished three innocent trashcans. It was going to be one of those nights.

e walked into the darkness of the bar's main room after some effort. Our climb up a long flight of mirrored stairs ended with a brief but vexing encounter with a burly bouncer who didn't believe Garrick was old enough to be on the premises.

"But here's my driver's license," Garrick said, nearly wiping the man's nose with the plastic square.

"Maybe they was faked."

"Maybe I'm old enough."

"It's just his boyish good looks that deceive you," Connie said before plunging into the bar by herself.

"Cut him open and count the goddamned rings," I demanded impatiently. With that I collected Garrick in my best I-am-the-teacher-here grip and propelled us past the bouncer and into the darkness of the bar. I was blinded as my eyes reacted badly to the sudden lack of light. Years too early for the sake of my mental health, I realized I was no longer as young as I once was. Garrick, whose nimble pupils adjusted more quickly than mine, began commenting on the splendor of the bar and pulling on my arm so he could see even more. I just wanted to see, period. Luckily, people were congesting the traffic flow and we were forced to stand still, bodies moving all around us. My vision returned. I always disliked the first few moments in a bar, even one I was used to. I always felt stared at, on stage. Perhaps it was a result of The Bloated Years before my diet. I'd haul my tonnage up the stairs and submit myself to the scrutiny of men whose lives were dedicated to the scrutiny of men.

"Where did Connie go?" I had to shout to be heard over the music.

"I think I see her on up ahead. I don't think she likes me much."

"Did something happen in the car?"

"Nothing in particular. She just makes me feel stupid."

He looked around us, turning full circle as he got a good look at the place. There were people pressed in all around us. Their clothes may have been multicolored before entering but it now all looked drab in the dim light. In groups and alone, men pushed past us, some talking, some silent, some staring just below our belt buckles, some looking at our faces, most with a drink or cigarette held protectively in the air. Eyes fixed on me momentarily, then moved on. Some returned for a second look, but I ignored them. It was too early in the evening for second looks. There was a mixture of sound: the clatter of chatter, overwhelming music with a steady heartbeat, a distant beer bottle shattering on the floor. Garrick turned to me with a wide, rubbery smile. "This place is great. It's so big. And clean. I thought it'd be grubby and smell like sweat and cum." He put a hand to his mouth. "Oops. Sorry."

"I'm familiar with the word. I'm even familiar with the smell."

"I keep forgetting. You're gay too. I'm glad." He hugged me and gave me a quick peck on the cheek. "Thank you for bringing me here. Should we find Connie now?"

"First, a drink," I said, not caring if we had little contact with her. I'd had about enough of her industrial strength personality. By asking Garrick personal questions and by taking it upon herself to force us to consider one another sexually she had taken possession of something we were both protective of, offering it up as flippantly as if it were the most trivial of matters. And what was this nonsense about drawing up a description of a perfect lover and coming up with me? Sometimes I was very, very tired of her.

Garrick and I pushed our way in the direction of the bar. We had to cut directly across the traffic's flow, which was counterclockwise around the perimeter of the huge room. Garrick had a hand on my wrist so we wouldn't be separated in the crowd. I could feel possibility flowing from his back. Our progress was halted by a rumba line of men — various shapes, sizes and levels of seductiveness — perhaps not drunk but certainly guilty of faulty footwork. I explained that there were many times when the bar got so crowded that the last millimeter of room needed even for impaired locomotion was filled and the entire room full of bodies ground to a halt. Human gridlock.

Garrick took advantage of our paralysis and got a more complete view of our surroundings. The widening of his eyes and the enthusiasm of his smile reminded me of my first encounter with a really nice bar. I'd grown up half-believing that all gay bars were filthy fire traps. It had been a relief to discover bars like Pay Days that were clean and safe.

We were standing on the second of three floors, usually the site of greatest activity. It was a long rectangle, with a dance floor at one end, surrounded by mirrors and lights and presided over by the inevitable reflecting ball. On the floor and throughout the bar there were nothing but men. And Connie. In the center of the room was a circular bar made of mahogany, with brass rails girdling it near the floor. Pyramids of drinking glasses rose in sundry spots. The bartenders were all young, extraordinarily good looking, and dressed as various fantasies from the gay male world. They were less than friendly, however. But they were beautiful so I could forgive them in part. I'd been a bartender myself before my battle of the bulge, and I knew that most customers did not deserve especially cordial service.

"What are on the other two floors?" Garrick asked, pressing against me as a lump of bodies struggled past. I wanted to thank them for the feel of his body against mine.

"Upstairs there's a smaller horseshoe bar. Some tables and chairs. But mostly it's empty for cruising. It's a lot darker than this. And look." I pointed above the circular bar packed with people where a ten-foot square of ceiling had been removed. Patrons of the third floor gazed over a railing at the patrons of the second.

"Double deck cruising!" he cried, genuinely excited. To be that excited about something again, I thought. It must feel wonderful.

"On the other end, though you can't see it from here, is another big opening where you can look down on the dance floor."

"What's downstairs?"

"During the day it's sort of a deli. Sandwiches and stuff. They try their best, bless their hearts. At night it's a quiet cocktail lounge. A lady plays the piano and sings. She's a lot like the sandwiches. She's had a terrible life according to those in the know. It's an older crowd there generally. And a lot of couples. It's nice to have it there just in case your ship comes in and wants to talk before setting sail."

Barechested men pushed their nipples past us, forcing Garrick even closer against me. He put an arm around my waist (thank god I'd lost that weight) and gave me a squeeze.

"Thanks for bringing me here, Harper. I was scared to come by myself." Then he kissed me on the cheek. I was going to kiss him back, but our path was cleared of bare chests and accompanying nipples, and we lurched forward only to be stopped a few steps later. The crowd clotted quickly. I suggested that Garrick stay put, that I'd go get our drinks. "Gin and tonic," he said, reaching for his pocket. "It's on me," I replied. I kissed his cheek and he smiled.

There was an overwhelming feeling of human presence in the room. Nearly claustrophobic, it somehow also managed to be terribly stimulating. There was constant physical contact; the senses weren't left unattended even a moment. Connie often complained that it was boring for her to be around so many unattainable men. Since they weren't quite so unattainable to me, I found the experience invigorating and a little frightening. She felt none of the sexual tension, her mind was not always on what might happen next. The same game-like intricacy heightened in me what it allowed her to relax completely. I reached the bar and pushed my way between two men to find a resting spot, elbows on the bar, one foot on the brass rail. I smiled at the construction worker who tended bar directly in front of me. He turned and walked away. I was ignored by seven classic gay male fantasies before finally being waited on by a mustached gymnast in tank top and trunks. As he made the drinks I looked up at the shadowed disks of faces looking down from the third floor. A man in a red shirt seemed to be looking back at me. Though a little startled, I met his gaze and held it. The gymnast tapped me on the hand and asked for money. When I looked up again, the red shirt was still there. We gazed at each other for a second time: he had a lethal second look. Then someone shoved me from behind. I was replaced at the bar and cast back into the crowd. I looked over my shoulder and found that Red Shirt was gone.

I slipped back in the direction of Garrick, wondering if Red Shirt would become a part of the evening's activities. But, no, he couldn't. I was with Garrick. Nonetheless, Red Shirt would make an interesting subplot to the tale I hoped to weave with Garrick. At that moment, the crowd once again became paralyzed, wall-to-wall people becoming a breathing advertisement for birth control. I found myself lodged between two handsome men. My arms were trapped in the air and the drinks perspired down my wrists.

"Sorry," I said to them. "I'm sure we'll be moving again soon."

But they weren't listening. They were busy arguing across the bridge of my nose. I peeped around my elbows at one, then at the other. "I can't believe you slept with someone else," one cried, obviously hurt.

"Why are you so upset? Even Mary knew another man."

"If you'd slept with God I wouldn't mind so much." I couldn't help but laugh appreciatively. He tilted his head in triumph.

"What do you expect of me?" the unfaithful one asked. He draped an arm around my shoulder. "What does he expect of me?" he asked.

"I'm afraid I wouldn't know."

"Who asked you?" his companion snapped.

"As a matter of fact, he did."

"Keep out of this," they said in unison.

"I like sex. That's all." He removed his arm from my shoulder, and I felt a bit of regret. "Just like any average guy."

"I think you're confusing average with common."

"Just because I have sex with other men doesn't mean I love you less."

The injured party addressed me. "What do you do with a lover who sleeps with your friends?"

"Be thankful he's not sleeping with your enemies?" I

offered, splashing scotch and soda down my neck. "Are you really sleeping with his friends?"

"Some of them."

"He must have a better set of friends than I do. Listen, you two. Lighten up. You're young. You're pretty. You're together. And you're standing on my foot. Just kidding."

Suddenly with a tremor that rippled through the crowd, bodies began moving again. One more wave of alcohol splashed atop my head, and I squeezed out of the not unpleasant grip of the feuding couple. I turned back to them and smiled. "Who was that mashed man?" But they didn't get it and I made my way back to Garrick.

I found him engaged in conversation with a tall, handsome, trimly dressed black man who affectionately brushed hair from Garrick's forehead. Neither saw me approach. Garrick said something; the man responded, a seductive smile spreading across his face.

"Here you are," I said awkwardly.

"I thought you'd been kidnapped," Garrick replied, taking his drink.

"Not me."

Garrick nodded at his companion. "This is Jeremiah. Jeremiah, this is my friend, Harper King. He teaches where I do. Jeremiah coaches basketball in. . . Washington?"

"Oregon. At a junior college. Hi, Harper." He shook my hand and smiled. He was very good at smiling. "I'm visiting friends before school starts next month."

He was likable enough. I just wished his interests in Garrick were not quite so obvious. His eyes were making veritable pilgrimages in Garrick's direction. "Did you play ball?" I asked.

"Four year letterman," Garrick answered for him.

Jeremiah asked if I'd played ball. Garrick laughed. I gave him a long look. "You think I'm not an athlete? I happen to have been an excellent gymnast. I won the state floor ex championship once." Garrick was obviously impressed. "I was on my college team until I hurt my knee."

"That sounds just like Jeremiah. He had to quit the Olympic team because he broke his wrist."

"The Olympic team?" I croaked.

"You were training for the Olympics?" Jeremiah asked.

"Uh. Sure. My injury came just before I was supposed to start really intensive training. That's the breaks."

"That's what the doctor said who set my wrist." Jeremiah chuckled and Garrick laughed along. "But now I'm healthy. Everything's repaired and working like a charm. So how about dancing with me now, Garrick? You promised."

"You mind?" Garrick asked me.

"Why should I mind?" My voice entered a new octave. With Jeremiah's long powerful arm around him, Garrick headed toward the dance floor, leaving me holding two sweating glasses. I was hurt. Why did he have to go off so soon? I considered pouting with all the stops out, but before I could Jeremiah returned. "He decided he wanted his drink after all. Am I busting up anything?"

"Such as?"

"Garrick isn't your lover, is he?"

"Did he say he was?"

"No. I just wanted to make sure you're just friends like he said."

"We're just friends like he said."

"Because I told myself when I first saw him that I had to have that boy."

"Such conviction is to be admired. Good luck."

Left alone, I surveyed the crowd. Nearly everyone was smiling. It seemed I was the only one alone. I felt like going home. Red Shirt reappeared, buoying my spirits somewhat. Maybe the evening wouldn't be a total loss. He was about fifteen feet in front of me, but we were separated by a half dozen bodies. He looked at me frankly and raised a hand, waving a subdued little wave in my direction. I followed him, inching my way through the crowd, excusing myself when I felt it was necessary, shoving past when those blocking my path weren't cooperative. I kept Red Shirt in sight for awhile, but my progress was poor. Once, he turned around as if looking for me. Then he disappeared. Another disappointment. The evening was a bust. If there had been an ocean handy I would have pulled a Norman Maine.

As I moved around the perimeter of the room, still on the trail of Red Shirt, I bumped into Connie and our friends, Brian and Ty, under a palm tree, one of five such growths inexplicably placed in the bar as some attempt at atmosphere.

"Brian just told a joke," Connie said, linking arms with me and pulling me near her. "Tell it to Harper."

"What kind of cloth is like a gay mystic?"

"I sincerely hope you're not going to say seersucker."

"You've heard it!" Connie cried. "Why haven't you told it to me?"

"I don't tell you everything, Connie."

"Well, start. Where's Garrick?"

"He's out dancing."

"Dancing?"

"Movement to music. It's very popular."

"Who's he dancing with?"

"A guy named Jeremiah."

"Oh, Harper, I am sorry," she gushed though her eyes were smiling. She let our friends in on the news. "Feel sorry for Harper, you guys. He's been jilted. Again. His beau is out dancing with somebody else."

"Garrick isn't my beau so shut up that kind of talk."

"Do you know what I think?"

"I wasn't aware that thinking was one of your talents."

"I think you're acting like one of the kids at school. Looking for someone else to blame when you fuck something up."

Brian and Ty leaned against one another, shaking their heads and laughing. "It's always so relaxing to go out with Harper and Connie," Ty said.

Connie turned on him with a sassy toss of her mane. "You be quiet. This is none of your business."

"It's your business?" he asked.

She didn't have an answer to that one. She asked Brian to dance with her. As they turned to go she turned to me and said she hoped I didn't mind if, while they were dancing, she got a look at the guy Garrick had dumped me for.

"I wouldn't want to deprive you of your entertainment."

"You already have. I wanted to see your face the moment you realized he wasn't interested in you."

Ty and I watched them disappear into the crowd, then he asked if I wanted to go stand somewhere else, so we wouldn't be found when they were through dancing. Sheepishly, I admitted that I did.

"Don't act like I'm doing you a favor," he said, bumping me gently with an elbow. "I can't stand her either."

Brian and Ty were my "bar buddies," for lack of a better term to describe friends I saw only in the confines of Pay Days. Ty I liked a lot, but I had mixed emotions about Brian. I felt in competition with him: which one of us would hook up with someone first? Bonus points were scored if we actually had an affair. We kept up with the sexual Joneses and, though we never spoke of it, we were obviously in competition. Not so with Ty. When I'd met him four years before, he'd been a pretty, pale, flighty, not particularly interesting boy of seventeen who one summer, with false ID and an impressive center of gravity outlined by tight shorts, became undisputed belle of the bar, the boy most likely to be found with his legs in the air. Then he'd fallen for George, twenty years older, the owner of a successful greenhouse, a nurturer of plants and people. Ty became a different, very special person in George's care, stable and kind and, like his mentor, a person who cared about other people. When George died suddenly the year before, I'd feared that without his stabilizing influence Ty would revert to his former habits. But happily my fears were unfounded. Ty seemed to become an even stronger person after George's death. He spoke with a confidence that made me imagine that in many ways George was still, and would always be, standing protectively by his side.

We were now under another palm tree, Ty, handsome in his worn levis and jacket, a hand slipped in a hip pocket; I, still made manic by my anger at Connie and disappointment in Garrick. Ty tilted his beer bottle at me. "I wonder why you and Connie are still friends."

"This probably isn't a good time for a rational answer to that one."

"You know how I feel on the subject of Connie." He'd never made it a secret that he was civil to her only out of respect and friendship for me. She said it was misogyny; he said it was good taste.

"She loves to see me miserable," I said.

"Then you do like this Garrick guy?"

"I like him, sure. But I'm not dying for him. I guess I read a little too much into our friendship. I'm pretty good at that. Jumping to conclusions is one of my favorite sports. Connie loves it when I jump to the wrong one and get hurt. I'm pretty good at that too."

"Don't you know why Connie reacts the way she does?" I shook my head. "You're smarter than that, Harper. George and I talked about you and Connie."

"I can't say I like being talked about. What did you say?"

"You're like Connie's husband."

"Excuse me?"

"You're just like her husband. You satisfy most all of her needs. What you won't or can't satisfy, she can get satisfied at almost any bar in town. She has a good set-up with you. She doesn't want it blown by you falling for someone else. That's why she's so happy when possible relationships fall through."

"I don't think we should talk about this any more." I suggested that we go to the bar for more drinks. I cut him off not so much out of loyalty to Connie, as out of loyalty to myself. Whatever accusations Ty made against her, he was also making against me for allowing her to behave in such a manner with me. As we waited for a man dressed in enough leather to make a Guernsey to pour our drinks, Ty wouldn't let the subject drop. "Know why she didn't like George and me?"

"Who said she didn't like you two?"

"Don't bullshit me."

He was right of course. She'd badmouthed their relationship from its inception. She was convinced that Ty was a gold-digger after George's money, and that George was in the affair only for the ego boost of being seen with a much younger man. She did very little to keep her suspicions to herself.

"She didn't like us because we were happy together. We were happier than she was. We had each other and she had no one. Except you and lots of one-night stands and screwed-up relationships. She was jealous of us and she gets jealous of you whenever it looks like anything or anyone new and exciting might be coming into your life. You maybe had a chance with this Garrick guy and she was jealous because she didn't have anything going for her. She was scared. Now she's not because it doesn't look like anything's going to happen with Garrick."

"Do we have to talk about this now, Ty? This is a place for public entertainment. This segment of the public is not entertained by the conversation we're having."

"I didn't mean to make you mad."

"I'm not mad. This just hasn't been a particularly sterling

evening and talk like this isn't helping much. Could we talk about something a little less soul-searching?"

"Looks like rain."

"Thank you."

We were quiet as we watched passersby. Some of them attempted to catch my eye; I allowed it to be caught by a few. I looked up at the third floor tourists gazing down from over the bar. There was Red Shirt again. He lifted his beer bottle as if in a toast to me. Then he turned and walked away. I told Ty I wanted to walk around alone for awhile.

"You are mad. I'm sorry, Harper. I shouldn't have said anything. George always told me to keep quiet about it. That you'd figure it out on your own."

"I'm not mad. A little embarrassed perhaps for not seeing it sooner."

"It's hard to see the smoke when you're standing in the middle of the fire," Ty said, obviously quoting someone.

"Winston Churchill?" I guessed.

"Smokey the Bear."

I laughed and kissed his cheek before moving toward the stairway that would take me to the third floor and, hopefully, an encounter with Red Shirt. Sex was the only thing that could salvage this badly damaged evening. I passed the dance floor, stopping momentarily to watch the bodies jerk and sway. The music seemed to lift everyone off their feet. Someone tapped me on the shoulder. It was Jeremiah. "Hi again," he said.

"How's it going? Where's Garrick?"

He pointed to the dance floor and shook his head. "He's a friendly one, isn't he? Five different people have asked him to dance so far and he hasn't said no to a one of them."

Just then I saw Connie's crimson hair bobbing toward me. I hastily wished Jeremiah good luck and moved along. I went up the stairs to the third floor. The desire for sex increased as my eyes adjusted to the even dimmer light. Perhaps it was anger and hurt and confusion redirected into my jockey shorts, or perhaps it was a permanent condition that I usually was able to keep at bay. Whatever it was, it was powerful. I wanted a man; preferably Red Shirt.

The crowd on the third floor was never as dense as that on the second. This was a haven for a varied group of folk: married men and novices who liked the deeper darkness; the truly horny; and the languishers, those who sat at small wooden tables strewn throughout the area, usually in couples and often attached at the lips. There was also a constant though not excessive flow of people just passing through, on a continuous circuit through the building. Most stopped briefly to gaze down upon the bar or the dance floor. I stood near the stairs and surveyed those around me. I didn't see Red Shirt. I walked slowly around the room, where sexual tension was heightened and body language took on more importance. One man winked at me while he kissed someone else. I looked over the railing at the dance floor. Flashing lights played across two hundred gyrating male bodies, some with their shirts off, many with their arms in the air, as they dipped and jerked to the pounding music. One of my favorite songs began to play, accompanied by an ear-splitting siren, both dying away as a disembodied voice — not unlike the warning voice of a teacher — reminded the dancers not to bring glasses out on the dance floor, not to dance while barefoot, and not to smoke while inhaling poppers. Several people booed at the chiding voice, but were drowned out as the music and siren were again cranked up.

As far as I could tell, Red Shirt wasn't dancing. But I did see Garrick. His blond hair askew and matted with perspiration, he was dancing with not one person but two. Unlike other dancers who seemed to be re-enacting the St. Valentine's

Day Massacre in fitful dance movements, Garrick moved with a small fluid swaying that perfectly filled the invisible boundaries of the music. One of his partners had apparently learned to dance by the *grande mal* method. His arms flailed, his ass jerked from side to side. His other partner, a handsome collegiate type, was more modest in his efforts, but was not nearly as nice to watch as Garrick. The collegiate leaned over and kissed Garrick, a long, full kiss. Not to be outdone, the convulsive aborted a pirouette (saving himself and those around him from possible physical harm) and sidled behind Garrick in a bestial manner. I pushed myself away from the railing so I wouldn't have to see any more. I bumped into someone behind me. I had already apologized before I realized it was Red Shirt.

"How you doing?" he asked.

"Things are looking up."

"I think I've seen you around."

"It could have been me. I've been around."

"It's crowded tonight."

"A little. Want to dance?"

"Sure, man. Why not?"

"My name is Harper by the way."

"Mine's Matt."

Under the bright lights of the dance floor, I could see Matt more closely than I had seen him all evening. I'd lucked out. Many bar boys are like impressionist paintings: better seen from a distance. His body was tight and solid. He seemed to dislike dancing, or he was just plain no good at it, for he moved in a self-conscious shuffle step. I put a hand on his shoulder and gave it a reassuring squeeze. In retrieving my hand, my fingers, impish things with minds of their own, grazed across Matt's chest. He stopped dancing. "Oh hold it," he said.

"Hold what?"

"Are you gay?"

"Pardon me?"

"I mean if you're not man I don't mean to insult you. But are you flirting with me?"

"I wasn't going full throttle, but I was putting some effort into it."

"Oh shit."

"That's encouraging."

"Listen," Matt said, "I don't mean to insult you but like don't flirt with me, okay? I'm not gay."

It's difficult to dance while taken aback, but I did my best. Of course he was gay. Had he just gotten a good look at me now and decided he wasn't interested? He grabbed my arm insistently, "I'm not gay, man."

"Fine. Whatever you say."

"You don't believe me?"

"Let's just say I'm surprised."

"But you believe me?"

"I believe you. Concentrate on your dancing. You haven't stepped on my feet in minutes."

For a long time we danced in silence. Matt's movements were even more tentative. He stared at me as if trying to read my expression, so I gave him nothing to read. When songs began to change, I took a few steps away from him, planning on leaving the floor.

"Hey," he called after me. "You mad?"

"Why should I be mad?"

"Let's dance some more. I'm just getting warmed up. Just because a guy dances with another dude doesn't mean he doesn't ball women. I'm engaged."

"A match made in heaven, I'm sure." I pushed my way through the crowd. Even Connie seemed preferable to this character. I didn't need to waste my time with someone who

cruises me then begs off with a sudden case of heterosexuality.
Matt caught up with me and pulled me around to face him.

"Where you going?"

"Back under a palm tree with the rest of the monkeys."

"Don't you want to dance with me, man?"

"No thanks, man."

"I want to talk."

"To a queer? Wouldn't that make you guilty by association?"

"Come downstairs with me and have a drink. There's no law says we can't talk."

Was it a weakness in me that made me follow him downstairs? Was it the teacher in me that made me willing to listen to his problems? Was it the hormones in me that made me hope there might still be a slim chance of our getting together?

We settled ourselves across a table from one another in the cave-like cocktail lounge. Raspberry Naugahyde glowed in the flickering candlelight. An aged spotlight did its best to illuminate an upright piano on a platform serving as a stage. Overhead fans seemed powerless against the stagnant air, blue with cigarette smoke. One table of patrons was a heavy contributor to the pollution. Either the group was ablaze or they were all chain smokers. As a waiter brought us our drinks, a heavy black lady appeared on stage. Someone applauded, but only briefly. She wore a green sequined gown far past its prime. She looked like a threadbare bullfrog. The flesh of her arms bounced and swayed as her fingers moved across the keyboard. Her voice was filled with gravel as she spoke more than sang her songs. But she meant what she said and one had to give her credit for that. Matt and I listened as we sipped our drinks and pretended the other didn't exist. I could sense he wanted to speak, but I didn't help him out. It took him awhile before he said anything.

"Listen, man, I don't want you telling people I'm, you

know, like gay."

"Whatever you say."

"You still don't sound like you believe me."

"It is a little unbelievable. I saw you looking at me across the bar. You even waved. You searched for me up there as hard as I searched for you. I do find it difficult to believe that you'd act that way if you weren't gay too. You were cruising me."

"I thought you were straight."

"Oh, come now. I may not flame, but I certainly flicker."

On stage, the singer was dedicating a song to the table of smokers. Cigarettes clamped tightly between their lips, they applauded politely, then returned to their conversation, ignoring her number. Matt asked me what about him seemed gay.

"Nothing specific. I wouldn't tell you even if there were something specific. You'd just try to cover it up."

"I told you before. I'm engaged."

"What's her name?"

He went through all of the same expressions my students went through when I caught them in a lie. "I used to be engaged," he finally answered defensively.

"Matt, there's a whole building here of people who are surviving being gay. You can too."

"There's nothing for me to survive."

"Have you had sex with a woman?"

"Sure. What do you think I am?"

"You know what I think you are. Did you like it?"

"Sure."

"Have you ever had sex with a man?"

"Maybe."

"Did you like it?"

"I didn't say... Maybe. Yes. I liked it."

"Have you ever been in love with a man?"

His face hardened. "Leave me alone, man," he cried. "Just leave me the fuck alone. I'm not gay. Anything I've done before doesn't count. It was my mistake and I'll pay for it. You just leave me alone."

He stalked out of the bar, leaving me to sit alone for a long time staring at the candle in front of me. I was exhausted. I'd had my fill of people. I left the lounge, then left Pay Day's altogether. It had been an all-around miserable evening: Garrick and his men, Connie and her jealousies, Ty and his theories, Matt and his hangups. I pitied me and my life. Standing on the street corner, I concentrated on the night around me. The air was still warm but it had a hint of autumn on its underside. I could feel change washing in on the breeze, almost hidden by the sounds of traffic and the smell of greasy food. I noticed two male figures emerging from their car in the parking lot across the street. One of them caught my attention. He looked too familiar. My heart skittered past a beat or two though I tried to tell myself that on top of everything else, my eyesight was failing. What if it was him? Would he remember me?

He saw me and it was obvious that he recognized me. He lifted a hand in a tentative wave; I wriggled my fingers ever so slightly in his direction. Traffic cleared, but he didn't cross the street. He just looked at me.

"Harper?" he called. I nodded. Then he crossed the street, in four or five running strides. "Harper... Harper..."

"King."

"Right. I'd forgotten."

"I'm not sure you ever knew it."

"My name is... "

"Mick Michaels."

"You remembered."

"I remembered."

"It's been a long time. You might hate me for all I know."

"I don't hate you. I won't push you out in traffic. Here comes your friend."

A fellow with reddish hair and the collar of his shirt standing straight up crossed the street. He looked sullen. Mick introduced us. His response was lukewarm. "I thought we were going to my place," he complained to Mick.

"I felt like having a drink. Now I'm glad I did. You can go home if you want to."

"Since we're here, we might as well have a good time. Nice to meet you, Harper." He slouched into the bar.

"Have you known him long?" I couldn't help but asking.

"About an hour. We escaped a boring party together. I guess I'd better be going in too." He hesitated. "How have you been? I've thought about you."

"I've been fine. I bet you never thought about me until you saw me standing across the street from you."

"No really I have."

His disgruntled companion poked his head out of the bar. "Are you coming in or not, Mick?" he asked.

"In a minute. Harper, I still have a few days left in town. Let's have dinner, okay?"

"When?"

"How about tomorrow?"

"Saturday? Can't make it. How about Monday?"

"Monday then. I'll call you tomorrow to get directions to your house. Are you in the book?"

"Always have been."

"We have lots of things to talk about. God it's good to see you again."

He went in the bar and I was left alone again, though no longer depressed. A car flashed past, heads poking out as obscenities were shouted at me. But I didn't care. Mick Michaels, at least temporarily, was in my life again.

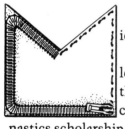ick Michaels.

I met him during my second year of college and, sophomoric me, waited until my third before my interest in him was finally consummated. I went to college on a gymnastics scholarship, the result of a state championship in floor exercise my last year of high school. I'd started gymnastics when I was eight because it was fun and it felt good; I continued because the stretching continued to feel good and the admiration of others for what my body could do felt even better. I found out later, with Mick's guidance, that the physical pleasure I got from gymnastics was in large part a sexual one.

Soon after I began my college gymnastics career, however, tumbling stopped being fun. I went from star status on an otherwise rather hapless band of athletes, to near obscurity on a good if not great collegiate team. This loss of prestige didn't kill the fun, however. Stoic practices, stringent rules and a coach my pretty teammates and I called *Il Duce* were the real assassins. Then a double back flip became an ambulance run and my career as a competitive gymnast was over. My knee was wrecked. Except for the loss of my scholarship, a month of constant pain, and crutches with minds of their own, I didn't rue the injury. I gladly hung up my jock and concentrated on other parts of my life.

Things were unfolding around me at a terrific rate; it seemed as if I'd been inside a cardboard box for seventeen years. Suddenly its drab sides were giving way to reveal a whole new world with which to get acquainted. I was Dorothy finally in Oz: life changed from black and white to technicolor. I learned about things I'd always been protected from, things everyone else already seemed to know. Not the least of which was sex. That was something I knew a bit about already, I must admit. I'd stumbled into two clumsy encounters in high school, more pitiful than satisfying. After the cast came off my leg, I wanted more than pity. I parlayed my still-fit body into five different beds, at that time a figure smacking of whoredom in my mind. There were a few hurried moments with men in a john, not on the beaten path of anyone but those in the know. Not romantic, perhaps, but nearly inevitable when one is seventeen, just discovering sex and too young to go to the bars. In retrospect, I'm glad those first few sexual experiences were little more than brief pantings followed by a lot of embarrassed cleaning up. They taught me the basics, leaving it up to Mick to teach me the complications.

Aptly, I met Mick in a gymnastics class. My doctor (always to be found with a stethoscope in one hand and a screwdriver — the drink not the tool — in the other) was certain that even though I'd never again tumble competitively, a moderate gymnastics class would strengthen my damaged knee. The teacher of the class was my old coach, the Francisco Franco of the pommel horse set. Despite my injury, I was far more advanced than my hopeless classmates. I was given a private corner of the room and a few mats on which to practice while the rest of the class tumbled, though usually not in any gymnastic sense.

Mick strode into class well into the second week of the

semester. Coach Doolittle confronted him and demanded an explanation. I couldn't hear the one given, but it didn't satisfy Doolittle, who, hitching up his sweat pants, asked Mick in an angry voice just what the hell he thought he was doing showing up for class so late. The discussion became tense, carried out between gritted teeth. We were all staring, hoping for a brawl, but we were not to be rewarded. Doolittle finally sent Mick off to the locker room to change into his "gear." My classmates returned to their hesitant handsprings. I watched Mick cross the room. He went to the door in that strange gait of his, as if he were pushing his way through an invisible crowd. He stopped before leaving, leaned in the doorway and examined us all. His gaze passed over me. He didn't smile at me, but I knew he'd thought about it at least. Then he flipped his gym bag over his shoulder and disappeared. I loved him from that first moment he hadn't smiled.

He was not as good looking as other men in the class. Some people didn't think he was attractive at all. But what do some people know? He was about an inch taller than me, but always seemed even taller. He had olive skin and small black curls that tumbled onto his forehead. Dense eyebrows jutted over steel grey eyes. In a way, he looked Cro-Magnon. I thought he was breathlessly beautiful; friends had specific complaints. He slumped. His nose veered. His skin looked unhealthy. He had too much hair on the backs of his hands. "There are so many men on this campus you could love," said a friend who suffered through my daily detail of Mick's smallest movements, "Why him?"

In class it was dangerous even to look at him. My physical reaction was not limited to a slightly racing heart and a feeling in my stomach as if it were making its first parachute jump; I had to be very careful about who noticed my shorts ballooning whenever Mick was near. In my little corner of the room, it wasn't too difficult to watch him surreptitiously, and in spirit at least I ravaged him several times. Sweating and gritting his teeth, he valiantly applied himself to all tasks at hand, taking success and failure with quiet humor. Often he talked to himself, sometimes he chuckled, most usually as he pulled himself off the floor. But he was beautiful as he stumbled about and clumsiness could be forgiven. He wore faded blue trunks, a white ribbed undershirt, and sweat socks with non-matching stripes. One, usually the left, drooped. Sloppiness had never been sexier. A thin gold chain circled his neck and against his dark skin looked phosphorescent. When listening to Doolittle's frequent harangues, he often draped the chain from his lower lip.

In the showers after class, though I was shy I wasn't stupid. As discreetly as possible I looked across the beige-tiled shower room at him with so many jerks of my head I'm sure I looked spastic. I was particularly fond of the sight of his thighs. Long and thick, they were a golden shade and covered with curls. His cock fit right in with the decor. It was obvious that Mick enjoyed being naked. He was the first person out of his clothes and the last to zip up. The other men under the steamy showers were an ample chorus line, but they surely weren't the stars of the show.

One day we had a particularly torturous workout. Doolittle seemed bent on breaking us all. He finally dismissed us to stagger to our lockers. Two guys vomited but we pretended not to notice. Many chose to skip a shower, choosing instead to stumble home and collapse in private. I was in no better shape. I throbbed all over, especially in my bad knee. I limped into the shower room so spent that I didn't look twice at Mick, who, pale from exertion, was, I managed to notice, one of the few who had opted for a shower. With my eyes firmly closed, the hot water cascaded down my body for nearly ten blissful minutes, numbing if not soothing its more painful spots. Finally feeling somewhat human, my first human thought was to take a peek at Mick. I was surprised and excited to find that Mick and I were the only two left in the shower room. He faced me, his eyes closed, concentrating on what appeared to be ecstasy as the water steamed and streamed over his glistening body. As I watched hyponotized, he took a bar of soap and began to slowly glide it over himself, leaving a slick white trail of tiny bubbles over his shoulders, across his chest, down his stomach and at last between his legs, his fingers disappearing as they soaped in more distant regions. With his free hand he reached down and lifted a handful of lather, which he spread on his thighs, those objects so nearly religious to me. With undulating strokes, he caressed the mixture into his flanks, fingers running through tangled hair I wouldn't have minded tangling with myself. The soap then concentrated on his cock, lifting the balls and edging me toward insanity. He shifted his hips in a slow downward glide and the cargo in his soapy hand began lengthening. I stifled a gasp and tried to decide what to do. Tackling him would lack a certain subtlety, I decided, and I opted on running away. I didn't want to be discovered pointing to the object of my desires without using my hands. I grabbed my towel and slipped and slid on the hazardous tile back to my locker which, for once, I was glad was tucked into a far corner of the locker room. Flopping face down on the bench in front of my locker, my towel balled beneath my head as a pillow, I could be alone with my fantasies and my body chemistry.

There was a wet smacking sound on the bench just above my head. Drops of water rained down on my head. A dark voice said hello. There was Mick, damp, legs straddling the bench, sitting just in front of me. My erection was crushed painfully between the bench and my body.

"Hello," I greeted his penis. I raised my eyes to Mick's smile. His hair was wet, the curls twisted. A drop of water clung to one lash.

"It was tough today, wasn't it?"

I was prosaic: "Uh-huh."

We spoke in short semi-sentences of the workout and our various pains. Mick asked me why I was off in a corner of the class instead of with the rest of the class. He listened to my story of the gymnastics team and my knee, but he didn't react. As soon as I finished my account, he told me his name.

"I'm Mick Michaels."

"I know. I mean I took attendance for Doolittle one day. Remember?"

"I guess. What's your name?"

"Harper King."

"Nice name."

"Thanks."

Then he asked me to show him the correct stance for a back flip. I was in no condition to stand up.

"Feet apart. Legs slightly bent. Don't tense them. Then think backwards."

"Show me. Don't do the whole flip. Just show me how to stand."

"Some other time maybe. My... my knee. It hurts. I think I better rest it."

"It hurts?" he asked. "I'll rub it. I give massages all the time. Roll over."

My cock was threatening to splinter the bench beneath me. I declined his invitation to roll over.

Still straddling me, he stood and grabbed my hips and flipped me over, revealing hard inches of incriminating flesh. He didn't say a word; he began to massage my knee. Gently and seriously he worked on it, rubbing and twisting ever so slightly, his ass hovering right above me.

"How's that?" he asked.

"Uh-huh." I was rather insulted that he hadn't noticed the state he'd put me in. He worked on my knee for a few moments more, then slapped his hands together. "There. That better?" I nodded. "Looks like this could use a little rubbing too." He squeezed my cock with a warm damp hand. Perhaps unconsciously, he ran his hand down his thigh, then briefly fondled himself as he had fondled me. Then, with a slight smile, he left.

I was incensed, I was in shock, I was in love. And I was in heat, putting my trembling hand to the use that Mick had so obviously been made for.

The next day when he walked into class, I was hit with a wave of embarrassment and anger. I didn't want to see him or speak to him. So, of course, he was assigned to the mat nearest mine.

"How's the knee?" he asked.

And just what in the hell did he mean by that? I wondered. I turned my back on him without an answer and did a simple cartwheel. When I landed, my bad knee crumpled beneath me and I hit the mat in searing pain. I was quickly surrounded by my classmates as if I were a three-car pile-up. Doolittle ordered Mick and another guy to transport me to his office where I could suffer in semi-seclusion. I draped my arms around their shoulders. Mick offered to carry me. Irrationally proud in my pain, I said I could walk quite well by myself, thank you, and let go of them. I was prone in a flash. Mick picked me up and carried me (more like a pieta than Scarlett and Rhett) into Doolittle's tiny office. I was placed on the only flat surface large enough to hold me, his cluttered desk. Doolittle slid the phone out from under my tail bone and called an ambulance. Mick asked me how I was doing.

"It hurts."

"Dumb question. Can I do anything?"

"You have a bullet I could bite?"

"Think my rubdown did this to you?"

"I doubt it."

"You can cry if you want to, Harper. Go on and cry." He extended a shoulder in my direction.

"I don't want to cry." Doolittle dropped the receiver on my knee and I let out a sob. I wept briefly in the general vicinity of Mick's armpit, then lay on the desk staring upward.

"You're good at gymnastics," he said.

"Better use the past tense."

"You want me to ride in the ambulance with you?"

"I can go by myself."

"I think they make someone go along. I'll do it. It'll be fun. I've never been in an ambulance before."

"Maybe they'll let you drive."

"I'll be very attentive. I promise."

When the ambulance crew crammed themselves into the office, Doolittle told Mick to hit the showers; he would personally accompany me on the ride to the hospital. I didn't even get a chance to thank Mick for carrying me to the office. I was loaded into the ambulance, Doolittle and his rank sweat suit at my side. Two beginning photography students who happened past made me the suject of their photo essay assignments.

A cast and more months on crutches followed. I was in the hospital for a week and had two operations. I had to withdraw from classes for the rest of the year. After spending months at my parents' home, we decided that for the sake of our collective sanity I should go back to school, rent an apartment and wait for the summer semester to begin. I went gladly.

I suddenly didn't feel like a teenager any more. That was fine with me, for being a teenager had not been my forte. Back at school I ran from experience to experience. I even had my first relationship that lasted longer than the time required to slip back into my clothes. His name was Steve and we raced to be the first to say "I love you," although neither of us meant it.

We just wanted to hear the words come out of our mouths. We were desperate to have boyfriends. I never really knew him, but I had a boyfriend at last and that was all that mattered. We played the roles we thought we were supposed to play, giving what we considered correct responses, clumsily experimenting with sex and love and all that comes with loving another man. Near the end of the affair, in the fall of my third year of college, I saw Mick again. It had been nearly twelve months, but I hadn't forgotten him. Neither had I forgotten the touch of his hand on me — not that I'd ever wanted to. It was the remembrance of it that had helped me while away the hours of my recuperation.

I had abandoned the physician who had recommended gymnastics as a cure for a weak knee, and my new doctor prescribed a moderate swimming program. So three times a week I trotted to the pool. Steve was about my size and an avid swimmer, giving me a complete trunk wardrobe. I padded from my locker to the pool with a slight rush of narcissism in red or orange or forest green trunks. Never much of one for aquatics, I pinched my nose and jumped feet first into the chlorinated water. My knee got stronger and I learned the backstroke.

One evening after swimming, while taking a shower, as if we'd never left the spots a year before, there was Mick showering right across from me. If anything he was more of everything he'd been before.

"Hi Mick," I said, having grown bolder in our year apart.

"Harper. I thought it was you but you look kind of different somehow."

"I'm not on a stretcher."

He rinsed and turned off his shower. Then he came over and turned on the one next to me, wanting, he said, to get a closer look at the scar on my knee, a toothy plum smile running along one side. I noticed that his inspection included more than my knee. I let him look as long as he wanted, and I enjoyed it.

"We have some unfinished business," he finally said.

"We do? I don't remember any."

"Sure you do." He laughed mysteriously and patted me on the ass. He didn't look back as he left the shower room. Any description of my reaction to his touch would be an underestimation. All thoughts of Steve, if they were ever in my mind, were booted out unceremoniously. I slipped back into my trunks — they seemed a little tighter — and started for my locker. I bumped into Mick, who now had a small swatch of white terry cloth the size of a place mat wrapped jauntily around his low slung hips.

"Ever been in any of the classrooms in this building?" he asked.

"I don't think so."

"Want to see something?"

Possible meanings of his question made me hesitate. Mick didn't wait for an answer. He grabbed my arm, led me through the locker room and out into the hall. I asked if we shouldn't get dressed, but he kept on walking. The towel was much too small for evening wear but he wore it in style. Forever slipping, it required constant readjustment. The top of his ass was exposed and his right thigh, retaining its old magic, flashed into view with every other step. He opened the door to a classroom and stepped in, beckoning me to follow. The shades were drawn and the room was totally dark save for a row of six aquariums all filled with fish and pulsating with milky fluorescent light. They hummed slightly as they breathed the soft sound of bubbles. Mick lovingly described each variety of fish to be found in each of the tanks. He distributed the dark green vegetation more evenly across the surface of the water with long and nimble fingertips. Readjusting his towel one more time he introduced me to his favorite, an angel fish with a vexing history of illness.

"Do you come here often?"

"Sort of. I used to come just to look at the fish. Now I study here and practice."

"Practice what?"

"My lines. I act. I was here rehearsing tonight. I have a terrible memory."

"What play are you in?"

"A short thing written by a friend who's into symbols. I play a suitcase."

"Can I help you pack?"

He laughed and put his arms around my waist, pulling me toward him. "Now," he said, "About that unfinished business."

"Which I know nothing about."

"I think you do. Don't you remember that first day we talked in the locker room?"

"Vaguely." He knew I was kidding. I gently touched his face with the back of a hand as he held me even closer.

"As I remember it," he continued, "You were lying ass up on a bench and you complained about a pain in your knee. It was a nice ass. But I massaged your knee." He leaned forward as if to kiss me but stopped just before our lips met. He whispered, "Don't you remember? I said that there was something else that needed my attention. If it still needs attention...."

He kissed me. I'd been kissed before, of course, but it had never felt like this. For a moment I thought I was tumbling right into his mouth. When it felt as if he were pulling away from me, I wouldn't allow it and tightened my grip on him. He had no objections. Our tongues dabbed and dueled; we bit each other's lips. He led me to a long table at the back of the room and we climbed aboard. My trunks were removed, Mick's towel discarded, and a tactile getting to know the lay of the land ensued. His body felt as wonderful as I had always imagined it would, solid and smooth. I especially liked the way his ass felt in my hands. And I finally had access to his thighs: long and strong, a gentle convex slope on the inside of each. Mick paid great attention to my chest and stomach, licking and flicking at my nipples with his tongue. I took his cock in my mouth and he swung himself around to swallow me. Talents I didn't know I had took over. We were quite a pair on that table, doing exactly the right thing at exactly the right time. Our mouths left a wet trail of harmless teeth marks. We wiggled and squirmed and held one another's hips as first he then I came with spasms impressive in their amplitude, as if this were our first orgasm — and for me it was, at least the first one that counted.

We lay side by side and recovered our breathing. I was awestruck; Mick watched the fish. I was in love; he was in a hurry. He got off the table and picked up his towel, saying that he had to be going.

"You're leaving?" I asked, not really believing that he considered this one of those quick sessions that I'd grown so tired of and could never consider this encounter to be.

"Somebody might come in. Thanks a lot. You were great. Maybe we'll bump into one another again." He wrapped the towel around his waist and headed for the door. Then he turned around, "Harper?"

"Yes?" I was nearly breathless waiting to hear what he had to say.

"Take care of your. . . knee."

And he was gone. I sat naked on the table, bitterly disappointed. At one point tears welled up in my eyes but the entrance of a janitor, shocked enough to go fleeing down the hall, got me back into my trunks and into the locker room. I hated him and loved him with a depth that was a revelation to me. He'd opened a door in me, invited me in, then left me alone to deal with whatever it was I found there. One thing he'd made me see was that Steve and I were a joke as a couple. I'd never come close to feeling with Steve what I'd felt in the too-short moments on the table with Mick. I left the pool, went straight to Steve's house to break up with him. He thought I had lost my mind, and maybe I had. I kept his trunks.

A week later I saw Mick again. Again we bumped into one another in the gym. He was just leaving as I was going in. I said hello, sounding for all the world like a heartbroken Sandra Dee. He asked if I wanted to go feed the fish. We went to the same room, lay on the same table and had even better sex. After it was over, I tried to roll into his arms to be held but he said he had to be somewhere in a few minutes. He patted me on the ass and said goodye. For most people, two such incidents would have been sufficient. I was in love with him and wanted him to love me back. It was obvious that all he wanted was sex. Sane people would have told him to shrivel up and die when he suggested that we go back to the room full of fish two weeks later when I passed him on the sidewalk outside the gym. But I wasn't sane. By the time we hit the room my erection was stretching painfully against my jeans and I practically begged him to hurry undressing and fuck me.

He was leaving moments after his last heaving sigh when I screwed up the courage to ask him why he left so quickly.

"I don't leave so fast."

"No. You always take time to cover yourself up before going."

"What do you suggest I do?" He wasn't intimidated by my hurt and angry tone.

"You could stay here and talk to me."

"What do you suggest we talk about?"

"Anything. Everything. Or we could go out for coffee or a coke."

"Maybe we could share one and each have a straw."

I was stunned. My lip began to quiver. To keep my mind off crying I began to dress. Behind me I heard him open then close the door. I turned, expecting to see that he had walked out on me. But he was standing there, watching me balancing precariously on one foot as I stuffed the other into my jeans.

"Let's talk, Harper."

"I don't want to."

"I do. What's on your mind?"

For someone who'd just said he'd rather remain silent, I was quick to blurt out that all he wanted me for was sex on top of a cold table in some room full of voyeuristic fish and I didn't think it was nice or fair or. . . it was here that the tears poured out. My, I must have looked foolish. But instead of laughing hysterically as he hurried into the sunset, he took me in his arms.

"I made you cry. I'm sorry, Harper."

"No you're not."

"Yes I am. I like you. A lot. Do you think I enjoy just running away from you? Do you think I enjoy not being able to talk to you?"

"You could if you wanted to."

"I can't."

"We could go out sometime. Are you embarrassed to be seen with me?"

"Of course not. I. . . I can't go out with you. I live with someone. A professor in one of the ology departments. We have a policy that we don't date other men."

"But we've had sex three times."

"Sex we can have. Just not a date."

"Is dating too intimate an act?"

"Basically."

"But Mick. That isn't fair."

"I know."

"I think I'm in love with you."

"Don't be." He kissed me quickly and left.

Five years passed before I saw him again outside Pay Days. I'd only been thoroughly depressed for six months. After that melancholia had set in for a year and a half. Even when I began teaching at Arthur, or perhaps especially after I began teaching there and realized that love was not going to be easy to find, I still thought of him constantly. He became a myth with me, a cosmic horny, someone I could never forget and never stop loving.

And now at last I was going to have a date with him.

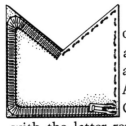onday arrived, but it took its sweet time about it. Before it did, though, I'd worried about my date with Mick from every angle. And I'd re-established relations with both Garrick and Connie, though the connection with the latter remained strained. She seemed to want an apology from me but none was forthcoming.

As I approached my house, my arms full of papers and my head full of daydreams, I saw Theresa Laugermann sitting on the front porch. Her fashion statement was forlorn: old khaki army fatigue pants that probably hadn't been in water since the invasion of Normandy, a too-large sweatshirt turned inside out, seedy tennis shoes with at least three toes exposed. Waifdom would have been an improvement.

"Theresa. What's up?"

"Thought I'd say hi. How was school?"

"The same as always, but I don't want your pity. How was suspension?"

"Boring. I walked around the mall all day. I saw lots of kids from school there. What's the green stuff on your shoes?"

"In the continuing battle against the forces of evil one of your classmates decided to paint the floor of the Reading Lab green. Do you like the shade?"

"They match your eyes."

"My eyes aren't green."

"I meant the ox-blood part. Can I come in ?"

"For a minute. I have a friend coming over pretty soon. I'll have to run you out so I can get ready."

I was digging in my pocket for my key when I saw the long box at my paint-spattered feet. "What's this? Who'd send me flowers?" Theresa shrugged. I made her hold my stuff so I could pick up the box and gently ease off the lid. Inside were a dozen roses, so red in places that they actually looked black.

"Those roses?" Theresa breathed. She placed my things on the floor and carefully lifted one flower to her nose. "Wow. Smell." She shifted the rose beneath my nostrils. I ransacked the box looking for a card but there was none. They had to be from Mick. Who else would send me flowers?

I hurriedly unlocked my apartment and we went in, my stuff tossed, forgotten, in a chair. I searched for my one vase, some somber thing I'd stolen from a funeral but had never used because I felt guilty. It was stowed in the back of a kitchen cabinet. Theresa watched me as I disappeared halfway beneath my sink.

"Thanks for standing up for me, Mr. King," she said.

"You're welcome. Oww. Nothing serious. I just bumped my head on the garbage disposal. I'm afraid my defense of you didn't do much good. But do me a favor and stay away from Maggie and her gang for awhile."

"I wanted to ask you something, too."

"What's that?" I emerged from under the sink with a heavy green vase. Going back to the living room, I tried my best to rearrange the flowers. My best was not very good. One after another tumbled to the table.

"You're not doing that right," she informed me.

"Very observant. Help me out, why don't you?"

Her hands were pretty and nimble as she quickly moved the roses about until they sprouted from the emerald vase in a lovely explosion of red. For a moment she looked triumphant, then she smiled at me shyly. I asked if she knew a lot about flowers.

"I know what looks pretty." With her smile and a faint blush on her cheeks as she looked at me over the roses, she looked pretty. I reminded her that she'd wanted to ask me something.

"Should I tell my father I got kicked out of school?"

"You haven't told him?" She shook her head. "Why not, Theresa?"

"I don't know what he'd do. He's always in a real bad mood. He might send me to Minnesota. He might do anything."

"I don't know your father at all, but my advice is to tell him. What if they call him from school for some reason? Do you want him to find out about it from a secretary or, worse, from Mr. Prynne? You'd better tell him."

"You think?"

"I think. Tell him it wasn't your fault. Tell him you had two teachers backing you up. Tell him to call me if he wants. That's what I think. And I'm also afraid I think you'd better be going. I've got to get ready. Sorry."

"That's okay." She shuffled to the door, her hands deep in the pockets of her fatigues. "Maybe I will tell him."

"You know him. I don't. Do what you think is best. Stop by my room when you get back from suspension." She nodded and opened the door. "Thanks for helping me with the roses."

"It was fun. See ya, Mr. King."

I went into my bedroom to get ready for my date.

Somehow I managed to run late. I stared into my closet then checked my watch to see if I had time to dash out and buy something new. Everything I owned made me look like a teacher. A navy blue blazer was the flashiest item I owned. I pulled it out of the closet, gave it a few harsh words, then set about deciding what to wear under it, hoping against hope that Mick wouldn't see it. I was tying my least authoritarian tie when there was a knock on the door. I gave my tie one last yank, nearly choking myself in the process, and, giving myself last minute advice on how to act, I threw open the door to find a man I'd never seen before.

"Did you get roses today?" he asked.

"Is this a survey?"

He removed his glasses and wiped sweat from his brow in the same movement of one hand. "I sent Tanya, upstairs, a dozen roses today but she didn't get them. I thought maybe they'd been delivered to the wrong apartment." He spotted them over my shoulder and strode on in. "What time did they come?"

"I don't know. They were here when I got home from school."

"You still go to college?"

"I teach."

"Oh, yeah. You look like a teacher. Did you think these were for you?"

"I assumed. There wasn't a card."

"Thanks for taking care of them. Tanya will return the vase."

He picked up the roses and began his trip back to wherever it was he had come from. He ran into Mick in the doorway. While apologizing, Mick slipped a rose out of the vase and hid it behind his back until the man was gone. He presented it to me with a smile and a smart nod. "Did you give that guy flowers?" he asked.

"They were delivered here by mistake."

"You can still smell them in the air."

He gave me presents: a bottle of wine and a plastic duck

with a corkscrew instead of feet. Despite my love of wine, I liked the duck the best and told him so.

"I was hoping you'd think it was funny. I didn't know if you had a sense of humor or not."

"I do."

He made himself comfortable and I got glasses, checking for spots first, of course. We spoke very little as the wine was opened and poured. I toyed with possible toasts should the duty fall to me, but he took a sip before I could even raise my glass.

"Well," he said.

"Well," I echoed back.

And that was that for awhile.

"I was afraid you wouldn't like wine."

I told him I loved wine.

"I didn't know whether to get red or white."

I assured him that rose was a fine compromise.

"Well," he said.

"Well," I echoed back.

I'm afraid I mostly just stared at him. I'd rarely seen him with his clothes on. His shoulders were surprisingly broad. It had been so long since I'd seen him at all that my reaction to what I still considered to be his beauty was the same as if I had never seen him before. His features, still dark and jagged, had settled into place, making him an imposing figure, in an unimposing sort of way. A few pounds too heavy to be described as wiry, he was dressed trimly in clothes that were obviously expensive. He, too, wore a navy blazer; it made mine look second-hand.

We finally began to talk, hesitantly at first, then with more confidence about my apartment, my neighbors and the ease with which he'd found me. I discovered that he lived and worked in Chicago. I told him I loved Chicago.

"You've been there?"

"I've spent a couple of weekends there. I had a lot of fun."

"It's a great place to live. Except in the winter. It gets dark real early in the winter. It's spooky. And kind of lonely."

He asked me what I did. When I told him, he made a face. "Really?"

"And what's wrong with teaching?"

"Nothing I guess. I just thought you'd be doing something different. Something. . . "

"More exciting?" I offered.

"Maybe. I can't picture you teaching."

"I'm good at it."

"I didn't say you weren't."

That ended conversation for awhile. We hid the silence by sipping heartily at our wine. I feared that we wouldn't be able to come up with anything else to say. Did I bore him because I was a teacher? I certainly bored myself.

Mick looked at his feet. "I thought maybe you wouldn't want to go out with me."

"Why wouldn't I want to?"

"Because I never asked you out before."

"You weren't allowed to as I remember."

"I wasn't very nice to you. I made you cry."

"I'd rather not talk about that. I'm not very proud of the scene I made that evening."

"I'm not proud of the way I acted either."

"Then we're even. Have some more wine and tell me the Mick Michaels story. I don't know a thing about you. Except you used to act and once had a boyfriend. And that you liked the gym."

"Since you don't know anything about me, how will you know if I'm making up the Mick Michaels story or telling the truth?"

"Would you lie to a man with whom you've lain on a table? Or in this case is it laid?"

His plane had taken off for New York City while I was donned in cap and gown, trying to engrave each word of every pompously repetitive graduation speech into my memory. He'd landed at La Guardia with seventy-five dollars in his pocket and took a cab straight to Forty-Second Street ("Like they do in the movies," he said, "But in the movies it doesn't cost them half of all the money they have in the world.") He emoted beneath a marquee until he realized that the play it advertised had closed the night before after only five performances. He dried his misty eyes and went in search of accommodations. He settled in a one-room apartment with two roommates in comparison with whom the view, a brick wall, seemed interesting. For three years he waited tables at night and auditioned during the day. There had been two commercials, but neither aired for some reason, and after about a year he'd gotten a week's work on a soap opera — he'd played a waiter of all things, dying on a Friday amid a crescendo of organ music in a restaurant fire set by the resident pyromaniac. His only other bit of success came when out of boredom he'd penned a very short, very dirty novel called *Leather Chaps*. A lover who had friends in low places got it published, its author listed as Mick Harper ("I liked your name so much I stole it," he said. "I'll give you a copy some time.")

Then a friend of a friend of a friendly trick offered him a job in a fledgling publicity agency. Things changed at last. The agency caught on through audacity and chance. For the first time he had money to spend, a job he enjoyed, and his self-confidence back. His foot was finally in show business, if through a side door. The agency had burgeoned to such an extent that a Chicago office had been opened the year before to represent the under-represented Midwest. Mick was now second banana in Chicago's office of Rising Star, Inc., and he seemed to be loving every minute of it.

"So now I'm in Chicago," he concluded. "Shivering next

to Lake Michigan. I like it. But it's different than New York. It's like living in America again."

"What are you doing here?"

"My boss is big on convention business. Little acts add up to big bucks. He wants to be kingpin for booking acts into conventions. So I'm here talking to the convention bureaus or chambers of commerce. And I'm checking out talent."

"We have talent here?"

"This is just a hotbed of genius. We'd heard a lot of good things about a gospel mime duo named Acts I and II. I caught their act yesterday. They don't say a word. They just act out hymns and parables with a lot of standing around with their arms perpendicular to their bodies. I also checked out an act called The Gesundheit Brothers."

"You're kidding."

"Four strapping lads who sneeze out old standards and the national anthems of all Western Hemisphere nations and selected Eastern countries. When we start booking State Fairs, these are naturals."

He touched my knee and suggested we head downtown to the restaurant. He named one of the most prestigious places in town and asked if I'd been there before. "Not recently," I answered. Never is not recently I figured. During the ride downtown, Mick, who hadn't seen the city in years, expressed amazement at its growth. "I don't believe it," he noted dryly, "Now you have to tilt your head back to see the tops of buildings." I was surprisingly defensive. I didn't especially like the city but I'd earned the right: I'd lived six lonely years in this big-city-with-the-small-town-heart. "It's no Chicago or New York," I answered, "But it has its moments."

"Don't you ever want to get out of here?"

"Maybe."

"I don't know much about you but I do know that you were made for someplace better than this. A big city. With excitement, a little danger. And complicated, interesting people. Just because this city has complex buildings now doesn't mean the people inside them have gotten any more complex. The architecture is interesting, Harper, not the people."

"I'll leave someday."

"When?"

"Someday."

He looked a little thin-lipped at my non-response, so I added, "Don't worry. It's something I think about a lot. It's just not particularly pleasant and I only want to talk about pleasant things this evening." I laid my hand briefly on his arm. "Okay?"

He smiled and said okay.

The restaurant was small, dimly lit and sufficiently proud to impress the hell out of me. The walls were red brick, unpretentious, the framed sketches original and highly competent. The atmosphere was intimate and tasteful. After I managed to forget the prices, I savored the food, probably the best I'd ever eaten. I think Mick realized how excited I was by the simple splendor. Several times I saw him just looking at me across the table, his fork poised halfway to his mouth. Candle flames danced in his eyes.

Over dinner we filled the air with reminiscence. We discovered that our paths in college had nearly crossed a number of times, though we scrupulously avoided talk of the times atop the table when they really had crossed. I regaled him with my standard anecdotes; I could tell that those he told me were from his tried-and-true category as well. As we pushed our plates away (they were immediately whisked away by an unobtrusive waiter) he asked when I was going to tell him the real Harper King story.

"What do you mean the real story?"

"All you've told me so far is ancient history. What about your life today?"

"What about it? There isn't much to tell."

"I don't believe you."

"Believe me, Mick. The life of a gay junior high English teacher, at least this gay junior high English teacher, is not exciting. It's pretty quiet."

"It shouldn't be."

"Why not? I pull it off pretty well."

"You know what makes it so dull?"

I paused until the waiter had placed coffee and liqueur before us to point out that I'd said my life was quiet, not dull.

"I stand corrected. Do you know what makes it quiet? Teaching." He looked triumphant as he said the final word.

"If you'd follow me around just one day at school you wouldn't say it was quiet. Or dull."

"But you don't like it, do you?" I shrugged. "Well, do you?"

"Not much."

"Then why do you do it?"

"I'm good at it. And there are parts of it I like."

"Such as?"

I found I was unable to explain. The complaints came easily enough, fairly dropping from my lips of their own volition. But the things I liked were so difficult to pin down. The way chalk felt on my fingertips. The way morning sunlight tumbled through my window and sprawled across my desk. The flicker of a student's face, however brief, that appeared when an answer offered proved to be correct. These and dozens of other nebulous reasons, easily overlooked, were what kept me tied to teaching. I was meant to be a teacher; it was in-born. Why else would I be moved by such minutiae?

"You're not answering my question," Mick said. What do you like about teaching?"

"There's a certain aesthetic pleasure to be gained from a well-maintained grade book."

"Now you're kidding me."

"Not really. For all its unruliness, school is neat and organized. We do this and then we do that. Go here, then there. All on a schedule. It's always different but pretty much the same. It's tidy."

"And quiet. And dull."

"And quiet and dull."

He raised his glass, swirling what was left of the liqueur around its curves. "Here's to a little more noise in your life."

After a quick drink at Pay Days our evening out began to draw quickly to a close. I felt sad as we drove back to my apartment, not wanting our time together to end, my meal sitting heavily in my stomach. As I fished my keys from my pocket outside my front door I wondered what would happen next, how we would part. Seconds away from any number of possibilities, I had no idea how I'd react to any of them. We went in and Mick stopped me from turning on the light. His arms slipped around my waist and we sank against one another.

"You want to see me again?" he whispered.

"Can I?"

Our lips met in a gentle, non-aggressive kiss, like a soft intake of breath.

"I go back to Chicago tomorrow," he said. "But I can come back. I'm not through with business here yet. Or pleasure. If you get my drift." His arms were still around me. My palms pressed against his chest. He kissed me, more boldly than before but still with a bit of hesitancy, as if I might pull away or slap his face. His tongue toured the byways of my mouth. Then he asked if he could stay the night. Many people would have said no. The word never entered my mind. I led him to my bed, though first I asked if he'd prefer a table. We lay kissing, touching, lightly tugging at one another's clothes. Mick kicked off his shoes and they hit the floor with two hollow thumps, not unlike the knocks on the door that immediately followed. It took a few moments and several more knocks to realize that someone was at my door. We jumped off the bed, tried to straighten our clothing, and flipped on the lights, guilt increasing our speed. I opened the door and saw a figure slowly moving down the stairs.

"Who is it?" I called.

"Me." Theresa Laugermann, her face in shadow, turned toward me. "I didn't think you were home."

"I'm home. What is it?"

"Nothing."

"Then why are you here? It's late. I have company."

"I didn't have anywhere else to go." She stepped forward into the light and I saw that one side of her face was puffy and blue.

"My god, come in here." I grabbed her by the elbow and steered her into the apartment. "What happened?"

She looked at Mick with embarrassment. "I... I fell down."

"On what?" Mick asked. "A moving bus?" He touched her face. She winced.

"This is Mick. And this is Theresa. Now tell me the truth. What happened?"

"My father. I told him I got kicked out of school."

"And he hit you?"

"He pushed me. I hit my face on the TV."

"Jesus," Mick whistled.

"Welcome to the dull world of teaching." I felt responsible for the injury; I'd told her to confide in her father. "Do you want to go to the hospital?"

"No. I'm okay. Really."

"Call the police," Mick said angrily, his eyes searching for the phone.

"No!" Theresa shouted. "Don't. He'd kill me. Please don't call the police."

"No one's going to call the police," I assured her. "But what do you want?"

"Can I spend the night here?"

Mick and I looked at one another, dismayed. I couldn't very well send her away. But it wouldn't be any easier telling Mick to go. I shrugged helplessly at him and told Theresa she was welcome to stay.

"I was just leaving anyway," Mick said. "I'll leave you two alone. I guess I'll see you next week, Harper. I'll call you soon. Theresa, I'm sorry about your... bump. I hope things work out."

"Mister?" Theresa asked. "Mick? Don't you have any shoes?"

He scooted through the apartment and retrieved his shoes from the bedroom. "I'll put them on later." I watched as he walked down the stairs and waved at me over his shoulder. I smiled sadly. He blew me a kiss and padded down the stairs carrying his shoes.

6

Theresa was gone when I dragged myself out of bed the next morning. The blanket was folded and a note lay on her pillow: she was afraid to be missing when her father woke up, she wrote; she'd see me later, and thanks. I hurriedly readied myself for school, stopping only briefly to consider calling Mick before he checked out of his hotel, but I talked myself out of it twice while dialing the number. I dropped my things off in my room at school, grabbed a cup of coffee in the lounge and went directly to Greg Prynne's office. Rose emerged just as I was about to knock. She stared at the cup in my hand.

"Did you know that caffeine is a drug?" she asked.

"One of its major charms. Is Greg in?"

"He is."

"I want to talk to him. And I might as well talk to you about it too. It's about Theresa Laugermann."

Greg stood near his file cabinet; both were strong and secretive, silent and ungiving. He gruffly asked what I wanted. As succinctly as possible I told him what had happened the previous evening. I avoided mentioning that Theresa had slept on my couch. "So," I concluded. "You've got to do something. You can't have her father batting her around like this."

In no uncertain terms they told me to mind my own business. They sang a duet, commanding me to silence. How did I know Theresa was telling the truth? Her damaged face was not evidence enough. She could have done it any number of ways, probably in yet another fight. She blamed it on her father because she was angry with him for some other juvenile reason, perhaps because he wouldn't let her watch television or hang out with her ruffian friends. When I insisted that it had been her father and that something be done to remedy the situation, they said that even if I were certain Mr. Laugermann had inflicted the wounds, still nothing could be done. It was a job for legal experts, not educators, and they weren't about to get the school's name dragged into the courts on circumstantial evidence. I mustn't, I was told, meddle where I had no business.

"Isn't it our business to help the kids when they are in trouble?" I asked, smelling smoke rising from my words.

"Our business is to teach them to read and write and behave," Rose answered.

"Not to testify in court," Greg added. "If he beat her up in one of our classrooms, then we could do something. Until that happens, I won't have my school involved in tomorrow's headlines. Case closed. As tightly as your mouth had better be closed about this, King."

"You're dismissed," Rose told me. But Greg had other plans. He told me to sit still. Then he leaned toward me, eyebrows drooping.

"I cannot underscore too heavily my distaste for what you did in this office last Friday afternoon," he said, making it sound as if I'd relieved myself on his desk set. "Damn it, King, we have to show a unified front with these kids. To sit in front of two students and contradict Mrs. McCormack and me is insubordination in it grossest form."

"Then the word doesn't enjoy the range of meaning I suspected."

"I don't need to remind you that this is the year you are considered for tenure," Rose broke in. "We must scrutinize your every action as a teacher before deciding whether we wish you to continue in your position. You realize, don't you, that one reason for dismissal, as well as for denial of tenure, is insubordination?"

"I realize."

"Now listen to me, King," Greg began threateningly.

"Now listen to me, Greg," I snapped, equally as threatening. "If you're suggesting that I keep quiet as the only way to guarantee my job, then we're going to have a very long, very talkative year. I'm not one of the kids you can push around. If I get pulled down for something like this, I can bring several other people down with me, at least two of whom are very dear to your hearts."

Though I didn't really know what I was saying, this seemed to hit the mark. It was obvious that they both felt I could possibly have something on them. I wondered what it was. Rose was immediately conciliatory. "Perhaps our words could be interpreted as being a bit too harsh. All we wanted to impress upon you is that in our battle against unruliness, it's best to voice our dissent in private instead of in front of the students who might try to take advantage of the apparent split in our attempts to keep the peace. I see that you've been insulted. That certainly wasn't our intention. Was it, Mr. Prynne?"

Greg lowered himself into his chair and was silent as he doodled with a pencil, the point of which snapped. "No. It was not our intention to insult you." He shuffled papers aimlessly.

What nerve had I accidently hit? "Now if you'll both excuse me," he grumbled, "I have a meeting with the superintendent very soon that I must prepare for."

I left my seat quickly. In my haste to exit, I spilled my coffee on Greg's carpet. I didn't apologize. I opened the door and was about to stalk out when Rose called my name. I turned and leveled a still-smouldering gaze at her. "Have a nice day," she said.

My destination was the nearest restroom where I could steam in peace. The boys within scurried without. I stood in the smoky air cursing Rose and Greg but most especially cursing myself for not saying more to them, for not being anyone other than myself. And I saved a little bit for Mick, who I missed terribly and who had made me admit that I wasn't satisfied with my life, then left me with my dissatisfaction. I made a fist and struck the tile wall.

"You're going to break it that way," someone said. "Your hand I mean." Dean Hopkins, one of my students, emerged from a stall, a cigarette trailing a spiral staircase of smoke in one hand. He wasn't afraid to be seen with it apparently; he even offered me a drag. "Troubles?" he asked.

"You're not supposed to be smoking, Dean," I reminded him needlessly.

"Sometimes you've just got to have one."

"Put it out anyway. But not just yet." I took it from him, looking away as our fingers touched. I inhaled deeply, but only once, for once was enough to make me dizzy. I crushed it out beneath my foot.

Dean Hopkins was the sexiest student I'd ever had in class. I could barely keep my eyes off of him, though I genuinely made an effort. The way he stretched to retrieve a dropped pencil, the way a strip of his flat stomach was exposed when he raised his hand, the way he looked at my body as if it actually belonged to a human being and might be something interesting to explore. He now stood before me, his t-shirt raised to mid-belly as he lazily scratched himself. Did I imagine it or was he looking to see my reaction? "Anything I can do for you?" he asked.

"No thanks."

"You look like something's wrong."

"Nothing's wrong."

"I'm good at helping out."

"I'll keep that in mind. You'd better get to class now. I appreciate the offer."

"Anytime." He ran his fingers through his shaggy blond hair. "I have a message for you from Theresa Laugermann."

"You know her?"

"She lives down the street from me. We're friends."

"Is she all right?" I asked.

"Her father hasn't hit her again if that's what you mean. Her message is that she's okay and she'll see you Thursday when she comes back to school. And she says thanks for letting her stay at your apartment last night."

"When you see her, tell her she's very welcome." A bell rang in the hall. "You don't want to be late."

"And miss class? Hell no. Hey, if I ever need to, can I spend the night at your place?"

"I can't imagine it would ever be necessary."

"You never know what will come up, Mr. King."

We plunged out into our mornings and I pinned my hopes on lunch to salvage the day. It didn't: baked beans decorated with Vienna sausage suspiciously resembling the cooks' thumbs; spinach, or so they said; grape-dominated fruit salad; and a carton of milk, slightly soured. It was into my empty milk carton that I shoved most of my meal. No wonder the kids used cafeteria food as ammunition. The sight of it was enough to spoil even the heartiest appetite.

I was sharing a corner table of the teacher's lunchroom

with Connie and Garrick. The latter, too, had little interest in his lunch. Connie, however, brought her meals from home; she was eating a chicken breast with a gusto that sent poultry grease splattering across the table. Garrick and I were amazed by the speed with which the poor bird disappeared. She noticed our attentiveness, put down the near-skeletal remains and wiped her mouth with the back of her hand. "So I'm hungry," she said. "I've had a rough morning. Sissy O'Connor had another seizure. I had to interrupt my impersonation of Miss Haversham to keep her from swallowing her tongue. Did you two get your extra-curricular assignments?" She'd been given an easy one, helping with career day in the spring. For several years she'd been in charge of the basketball pep girls. But she'd run afoul of Greg, who complained that her charges' routines were rife with the suggestive.

"I'm on the planning committee of the Halloween party," I said.

"Me too!" Garrick cried. "What do we do?"

"Just choose the right kids. They do most of the work."

"At first I thought I'd been assigned to build the float for Arthur's contribution to the high school's homecoming parade. But that's what Elmo Dobson got."

"Are they still confusing your mail with his?"

"All the time. When we got our paychecks I almost had a heart attack. Do you know how much he's making?"

"Much more than he's worth, I'm sure." Connie turned toward the door as Rose made an entrance. Rose surveyed the room, where various members of her department sat ignoring their meals. "Hello, troops," she called cheerily. Her smile faded when she saw me, and she seated herself, immediately attacking her wienies and beans. Connie leaned across the table toward me and asked, "What's wrong with her? You two fight again?"

"Not really a fight. More of a disagreement."

"You don't seem too upset about it. Usually you stomp around full of all sorts of wonderful bile. You in a good mood?"

"It's taken some effort, but yes, I think so."

"How come?"

"I had a date last night. It was very nice."

Connie's eyes narrowed. "Who'd you go out with?"

"His name is Mick Michaels. I kind of went out with him in college for awhile."

"Now he's living here?" Garrick asked.

"He was in town on business. He left this morning."

"So another slam bang etcetera in the life of Harper King," Connie sighed. "Tough luck, cookie."

"It wasn't like that at all. There was no slamming and banging. As for etceteras, he's coming back next week to see me."

Connie's face fell, but I chose to ignore it. Garrick wanted to know all about Mick and our date. I obliged, leaving out the specifics of our past acquaintance. He found it all very exciting, saying that he hoped it was the beginning of a romance for me.

"Don't worry," Connie said. "I've known Harper for a long time now. Nothing will come of it."

"Leave him alone, will you?" Garrick cried. "You're supposed to be his friend. All you do is sit and make fun of him. What's the matter with you?"

Connie stiffened in her seat. When she spoke, it was slowly, as if her voice were barely under control. "I'd explain it to you, but children rarely understand the workings of the adult world. As for you, Harper, you're a fool. I'd love to stick around and describe the nature of your foolishness in all its many facets, but it isn't pleasant in here any more."

Red hair waving behind her like so many ruddy spider webs, she stalked out of the cafeteria, shoving aside any chairs and people who might be in her path. "I can mark another friend off my list," Garrick said. "What's wrong with her anyway?"

"Who knows? I used to think I knew her really well. Now I don't understand her at all. She's changed. Once she was nice and funny all the time. Now, well, you can see how she is a lot of the time now. Sometimes I think our friendship is drawing near its conclusion. But then I feel guilty and tell myself I'm being selfish. She needs a friend."

"She needs a rap across the chops. The way she acts, who can be expected to be her friend?"

"We all have our troubles."

"I know that as well as anyone. I have troubles but I don't make life miserable for everyone around me."

"You only make it miserable for yourself?"

"Something like that."

"I've noticed you kind of moping around the last few days. What's wrong?"

He ducked his head and blushed slightly. With his fork he made one last swipe at his meal. "I feel sort of lonely," he said. "I feel silly admitting it."

"Being lonely is nothing to feel silly about. I've done it for years and never once felt silly. What are the particulars? New job, new city? Lost friends and youth?"

"Are you making fun of me too?"

"Not at all. It's natural to feel that way once you leave school and start to work in the real world. I went through it. With a vengeance. What about the people you met at the bar the other night? You seemed to attract a lot of attention."

"I got a few calls from them, but... I don't know. They're pretty advanced for me."

"The first ones to pounce are usually the pros."

"I need someone as naive as I am. I mean, I know what to do and how to do it, but I'm not a pro. Some of those people at the bar were attracted to me just because of my amateur standing. Besides, I'm not lonely for sex. I can get that anytime I want. It's everything else that I want."

He spoke softly of his romantic experiences in high school and college. There were few to speak of. He again told me of his relationship with a girl named Stacy who he'd planned to marry but who'd married his younger brother instead. Like many gay boys on first arriving at college, he'd developed a crush on his roommate, a senior named Carlos, a gentle Latino who was easy to talk to, a dangerous trait in any man. But, alas, Carlos seemed to have an incurable attraction to women. Imagine Garrick's surprise when the night before Carlos graduated, he'd been invited into his bed. Though Garrick had written him several letters after they'd parted, he'd never again heard from Carlos. Since then, romance had not been Garrick's strong suit, though he'd had his fair share of sex. His longest relationship had lasted only two months. Most of them had a duration of only a few weeks. He longed for love, but was at a loss to define what it was exactly.

"Sounds like my story," I told him.

"But now you have Mick."

"One date doesn't give me proprietorship. I was always philosophical about being loveless. I figured love is like a big pitch-in dinner and I am one of those salads that all look alike and are passed over for the meat and potatoes further down the line."

He laughed for a moment, but once again became somber. "How can I expect to meet anyone when I'm teaching here? I thought after you started a career you meet all sorts of interesting people and were faced with all sorts of neat ... I don't know the word."

"Possibilities?"

"Good enough. But look at the way things are. The people we work with are dull and boring. The men either married or dull or both. You're the only interesting man here and right now I need you as a friend more than anything else. Where's the excitement, Harper? I'm so exhausted by the time I get home that I have to take a nap. When I get up I have to get ready for classes the next day. Then it's time for bed. When I do go out, people only talk to me long enough to ask me their place or mine. Is this what I have to look forward to for the rest of my life? I don't think I can take it."

"Things will get better," I said, not quite convincingly. "One day you'll have your back turned and love will plow right into you. So to speak."

He asked if we could take a walk. As we passed Rose's table, I nodded gravely. She bent over her food with more intensity. We walked through the echoing halls to a little-used exit by the gym. Several students had to be shooed indoors, their contraband cigarettes and joints hurriedly extinguished, before we could settle ourselves on the concrete steps. Our view was of the football field, more brown than green, with two small figures running across it, abruptly halting before taking flight again. Beyond the field a clump of trees was already turning shades of orange and red. Through the trees was a gray strip of highway. Cars and trucks flashed past, sun ricocheting off their windows, bursting into view from behind one group of trees only to seek shelter seconds later behind another. The pull of movement, the sense of travel and escape were strong, so strong that I had to force myself to look at Garrick to break the spell. He, too, stared out into the distance, a wistful look of envy in his eyes for those out on the highway free to come and go as they pleased.

"I got a letter from my mother the other day," he said. "She doesn't think I'm happy. She wants me to come home to Pittsburgh after this year. She says she'll pay my way to law school."

"Are you going to do it?"

"I don't know. I haven't really given teaching a chance, have I?"

"Probably not."

"But you've been teaching a long time now. You tell me. Is it worth sticking it out for?" I was silent. With a sigh, Garrick rested his head on my shoulder. "I think you've answered my question."

I stroked his hair. "You deserve better than this. You'll get it someday."

"Are you sick, Mr. Dobson?" Rose asked from behind us.

He jerked his head off my shoulder, unable to hide his fright. "You should have been here a few seconds earlier, Rose," I said. "You missed Garrick's impersonation of a kid in his class who fell asleep during a spelling test. He slumped right over onto the next kid's shoulder."

"I'm sure it was amusing." She seemed suspicious. "Nevertheless, Garrick, show time is over. The bell rings in two minutes and I believe you have a class to teach." He leaped to his feet and without saying a word hurried into the building. I stood too, though more slowly. Rose remained in the doorway, blocking my path. "Stay away from Garrick Dobson," she said. "He's young and impressionable."

"And I might make the wrong impression?"

"Something like that."

"Who Garrick is friends with is hardly departmental policy. He does as he pleases."

"And does it please him to put his head on your shoulder like some spooning schoolgirl?"

"I told you he was . . . "

"I know what you told me. And I'm telling you. Leave Garrick Dobson alone." She slammed the door in my face. I heard the click of the lock. I began to walk around the building. Behind me a horn blew on the highway. I realized the road was one that led to Chicago. And Mick.

hey light bowling alleys the way they light schools: lots of overhead fluorescents seeping down to jaundice cheap wood. As I entered the Pin-E-Lane Bowling and Family Recreation Center, I decided the building's personality was not unlike that of an aircraft carrier, without all the cute men in uniform of course. No wonder Rose had selected this as the site of a mandatory morale-boosting get-together for her English faculty: bowling alleys were so Rose.

And I was already late. Just as I had been grabbing my keys to dash out the door, Mick called to say hello and to commemorate the one week anniversary of our date. He asked me about Theresa. I was able to tell him she was safely re-enrolled in school, her face was healed and her father's anger apparently cooled. As a punishment for my impertinence, Greg had transferred her to my class where I would have to deal with the actions I had so willingly endorsed. As I'd suspected, she was a bright student, if not one in the traditional mold. She still seemed rather alienated from her classmates, the only one she talked to being Dean Hopkins who sat next to her. More than once a period I had to break up their little whispered tete-a-tetes. Otherwise she was a pleasure to have in class.

"Tell her hello for me," Mick said. "Maybe next time I'm in town she won't interrupt the proceedings."

"When are you coming back?"

"As soon as I can. Things are up in the air. Do you miss me?"

"I don't really know you."

"But do you miss me?"

"Yes, I do."

I told him I had to go bowl. I had to tell him three times before he'd believe me. Don't go if you don't want to was his advice when I told him I wasn't looking forward to the ordeal. But, I said, I had to go; one didn't cross Rose too often if mental and physical well-being were one's goals, and I had already tried her limited patience.

"You need some assertiveness training," Mick said before saying goodbye.

"Will you be my tutor?"

"If provided with certain fringe benefits."

"I'll see about that."

"I can be very persuasive."

Then why hadn't he persuaded me to stay home, I wondered as a half-acre of lanes yawned before me. Figures in stretch pants defied gravity and good taste as they wobbled and squatted and shouted at retreating but unheeding balls. Over their heads, tiny projectors flashed scores on the wall, box after box of slashes, x's and ill-fashioned numerals, scrawled by monstrous hand shadows armed with pencils the size of small stumps.

Rose was suddenly at my side. "We're on lanes sixty-one through sixty-four," she said.

"You mean there are sixty-four lanes here?" I asked. I had

assumed in my innocence that our government protects its citizens from such things.

"There are seventy-two altogether. Isn't it magnificent?" Her arms orbited about as she presented Pin-E-Lane for my approval.

"Quite impressive. I've always admired bowling alley architecture. And, of course, the decor. Early Congolium, isn't it?"

She didn't seem to hear me. "Shall we find the others? But don't forget your shoes."

I was steered to a desk belonging to a man in a fuchsia shirt with "Wildcat Striker" stitched above a pocket. While we waited in a short line for the shoes, Rose elaborated on the building's many features: One hundred pinball and video games, thirty-two pool tables, shuttle bus and babysitting services, outside sanitary facilities for campers, and regular bowling tour groups. Over the summer, Rose had gone on a five-day tour of the great lanes of the Napa Wine Valley. On Sundays, Pin-E-Lane held three fifteen-minute non-denominational church services in the TV room. "Of course, *real* believers don't bowl on Sunday," she said. "I hope you're wearing socks. No matter how strict we are about who gets in here, you never can be too careful, if you know what I mean. You can never be too concerned about your feet."

I was saved from a discussion of podiatric health when the Wildcat Striker pushed a pair of maroon and green saddle shoes into my hands and demanded a dollar. Rose wanted to know if this was the way I dressed outside of school. I looked down at my softest flannel shirt, faded jeans and tennis shoes and asked her if there was something wrong. "Aren't you a little old to be wearing sneakers?" I ignored the remark and pretended to be moved by the ornate snack bar. Rose caught me by the arm and swung me around to face her. "Harper," she said, "we haven't started this year on very firm footing. That bothers me. A team divided is a team defeated. Let's call a truce. I'm sorry if I've stepped on your toes. I love my job and sometimes, I've been told, I go overboard." What had come over her? Did bowling have this effect on her? Perhaps we should install a couple of lanes at school, I thought. "Yes, Rose," I replied non-commitally. I wasn't convinced of her sincerity; this could just be a new tactic to trip me up.

We reached our kegling colleagues. Crowded around four lanes was the staff of the English Department of Chester A. Arthur Junior High School. An odd crew at best, they were not at their finest in a bowling situation. Carrying balls as an expectant mother carries a long-overdue baby, they crouched in various painful-looking positions, some falling to the floor after an especially haphazard fling. I was surprised to see even Connie on her knees, beating a narrow strip of tape on the floor while a red penalty light flashed frantically above her.

"I did not foul!" she screamed. "What the hell is wrong with this thing?" A sprig of dried flowers she had placed in her hair as decoration fell to the floor. She beat on it with her fist. Rose told her to get off the floor. 'You shouldn't call attention to your behind," she said.

"I've been told by many men that my behind is my best feature," she replied good-naturedly as she hauled herself to her feet. "Which doesn't say much for the men I hang around with. Or my other features." She smiled and waved at me. The tension between us had cased somewhat but still a resentment of me and my talk of Mick flared at odd moments. Being friends with Connie was like a having a relationship with mercury; one never knew in what direction it would scurry next. I spoke briefly with some of the others. I was friendly with all of them, as they were with me, but we really couldn't have cared less about one another. Before going into teaching I'd heard about the comaraderie of faculties everywhere. It was not the case at Arthur.

Rose pulled me over to the fourth of our four lanes and explained that she'd divided us up into teams. Because I was late only two teams had been able to begin.

"Teams?" I asked as I hurriedly changed shoes.

"Rose thinks competition is good for the soul," whispered Bev, sitting next to me. She was middle-aged but still had an endearing schoolgirl's giggle. "Rose takes bowling very seriously."

I wasn't pleased, then, to discover that Rose and I were on the same team. Garrick, who still hadn't shown up, would be on our team too. We'd be bowling against Bev, Rick (the tennis coach whose legs blooming from gym shorts each fall added an extra headiness to the air), and decrepit Agnes Winchester, already alive the day God created the first prepositional phrase. She was wearing a long cotton skirt and bobby socks, her glasses dangling from a chain around her neck. Slow even in her more sprightly moments, she seemed to go through life by osmosis.

Rose told me to bowl first for our team. I'd been bowling three times in my entire life, always against my will and never with any distinction. My method of delivery consisted of a cursory glance at the pins followed by a disinterested toss of the ball, usually resulting in a few toppled pins, victims of sheer force. I hoped Rose would let that suffice. I let go of the ball with a pop of my fingers and promptly deposited it in the gutter. I received a long round of applause from my colleagues. "I hope that doesn't persist all evening," Rose commented dryly.

"And I hope you realize that life is one disappointment after another."

"Throw it harder this time. And keep your thumb up."

So I sent it flying again. The ball skidded across two adjacent lanes and bestowed upon Connie the first strike of her life. She was thrilled, but not so with Rose, who shook her head and refused to look in my direction.

The competition proceeded. For my team it was a debacle. Two against three in the first place; when one of the two was Harper King, things were really bleak. Bev, it turned out, was on a church team with Rose, the Holy Rollers by name to no one's surprise or amusement. Rick, who had brought his wife and new baby to watch our antics, was capable of rocketing the ball with shattering efficiency. Poor Agnes Winchester was worse than anyone I'd ever seen or heard of. Like the child several lanes down, she placed the ball at her feet and gave it a modest shove. When it did not veer into the gutter — a rare occurence indeed — it moved so timidly down the lane that it barely moved a pin. Several times it stalled halfway down the lane and someone, usually I, had to hurry down to retrieve it. Rose concentrated very hard on her own game, intently staring down the lane, adjusting her wrist band, altering her stance. Seldom did she come away with anything less than a spare. With muttering and musing and self-castigation, she penciled information into a spiral notebook, reminders to aid her in improving her game. When not pulverizing the pins with her fiery speed ball or making self-help notations, she knitted a blue sweater for her grandson and told me to concentrate on my game, whatever else I did remembering to keep my thumb up.

While awaiting my turn I wandered around, chatting and catting with the others, sipping Connie's Coke, conveniently spiked, and hoping that Rose would twist her ankle or something more vital, causing her to withdraw and go the hell home. Sometimes I talked to Rick's wife or played with his baby, an egg-shaped creature with a talent for blowing bubbles and in possession of eleven fingers, though no one made mention of it aloud.

The first game was over by the time Garrick arrived, out of breath and full of apologies. "Things came up, Mrs. McCormack. I got here as fast as I could. I'm sorry. I'm so sorry."

"I don't like tardiness. I hope this doesn't happen again."

"It won't, Mrs. McCormack. I promise."

I went with him to get his shoes from the Wildcat Striker. I told him not to worry about being late. "You've missed nothing of importance. So far the highlight of the evening has been Connie running down the lane because one of her new fake fingernails fell in a hole of her ball."

"I hate having Rose mad at me. Especially after her finding me with my head on your shoulder last week."

"Believe it or not, she called a truce with me. Said she was tired of fighting."

"Do you believe her?"

"Part of me is suspicious. But part of me just wants all the arguing to end. I'll have to wait and see. How come you were late?"

"It's a long story. I don't have the energy to go into it now. A dollar? It costs a dollar just to rent a pair of shoes? I hate bowling."

Bless him, he turned out to be just awful, much to Rose's dismay. "Who taught you to bowl? Harper? Keep your thumb up! Your thumb!" Her advice was to no avail. Throughout the game he was preoccupied. Silent and withdrawn, he didn't respond even when Agnes Winchester picked up his much heavier ball by mistake and was immediately pulled to the floor in a heap. When the game was over, he ran to a phone, returning even more preoccupied, just in time for the third and final game. "What's wrong with you?" I asked as we sat side by side amusedly watching Rose adjust her stretch pants.

He sighed. "I have love problems."

"Love? I thought you were lonely."

"That was last week. I met someone a couple days ago.

And I was late because we were busy having a fight."

"Already? This sounds intense. Who is it?"

"It's a secret."

"You're kidding."

"I just don't want to go into it now. Do you mind if I don't tell you for awhile?"

"Of course I mind. But I'll let you have it your way. Do I know him?"

"I can't really say."

Connie plopped down beside us and removed a shoe. "My feet are killing me," she said. "What are you two over here whispering about?"

Garrick began to explain. "I was just telling Harper that I'm having . . . "

I nudged him and gave him a wary look. "He was telling me that he's having a terrible time with his bowling. I told him to imagine ten little Roses down there waiting to be obliterated. I find it easier that way.

Connie retied her shoe. "I'll try that too. Though they're shaped more like me."

"You better get back to your team," I told her. "They're dusting the gutters in anticipation of your next delivery."

When she was gone, Garrick asked why I'd lied to her. "Like your new love," I explained, "it's a long story, better discussed at another time. For now let's just say that it's easier if Connie doesn't know everything about everyone." Was this a signal of an official change in our relationship? Or had it been the previous weekend when Connie had canceled our Friday night engagement for the first time I could remember; her only explanation was that she couldn't make it.

Luckily, bowling soon ground to a halt. We looked comically childish as we searched for our shoes shoved far under our benches. Agnes Winchester lost hers, poor thing, and Rose had to be queried about the possibility of Agnes wearing her bowling shoes home. After that crisis was solved — a four-year-old was found in the TV room clomping around in Agnes's pumps — Rose suggested that we rally at a local pizza parlor, the culinary equivalent of a bowling alley. Most everyone begged off, including Garrick, who left in a rush to resume his battle with his new and unnamed lover. I vigorously declined the invitation, using everything from papers to grade to the demise of yet another goldfish as an excuse. Rose, however, would have none of my excuses. "You most especially should go, Harper," she said with just a hint of threat in her voice. "This is your tenure year and you mustn't go it alone. A successful tenure reflects a successful department. And a successful department is a cohesive department."

And a cohesive department, I assumed, pigged out on pizza en masse. I was trapped. I resigned myself to being one of the six people finally coerced into meeting at the nearby den of dyspepsia: besides Rose and me, Connie, Bev and Agnes Winchester would be coming along. Also in the group was bland and balding Harvey Wilcox, and Rick, whose wife had insisted, much to his rue, that she take the baby home alone so he could go out with his friends.

We were silent as we waited for our pizza. Rose was quite human, even when we ordered beer, which, she'd once commented, was the first step toward tainted lives. To break the pall enveloping us, she began asking questions about our personal lives, not in a prying manner, but with interest and sympathy where interest and sympathy were warranted. I eyed her with even more suspicion, but she really seemed to care when Agnes Winchester slowly detailed the need for more roughage in her diet. Her eyes even twinkled merrily when Connie passed Agnes a basket of breadsticks and told her to eat them in good health. "Harper, I'm ashamed of myself," she said between sips of her cola, "But I know very little about your family life. Do you have many brothers and sisters?"

"Five. They're spread out all over the place. All married. Mom spends her time between Illinois where I grew up and Florida. My father died my last year of college."

"I'm sorry."

"Dad wasn't very happy about it either."

"Oh, Harper!" Rose laughed. "Sometimes your sense of humor *is* wicked."

I told them that my entire family was made up of teachers. There were appreciative murmurs from my dining companions. It was as if I'd said we'd all quaffed from the Holy Grail. "Then you get your teaching abilities naturally," Rose commented to my utter astonishment. Across the table from me, Connie choked on her beer.

The arrival of two huge pizzas curtailed my description of my family and our collective educational bent. Rose's chumminess had broken the ice; we all actually conversed as we ate. I sat across from Connie and in between Rick and Agnes. Though I spoke briefly to Agnes (in response to her asking me if I were a new teacher at Arthur) and to Connie (who made a terrible face and refused to say another word to me when I mentioned Mick's name), I spent most of my time chatting with Rick. Connie wasn't pleased by that either, for she had been ferociously flirting with Rick, but to no avail. So she turned her charms on Harvey Wilcox sitting next to her in all his dreariness. Although Harvey had long been an object of her ridicule ("He's shaped like an onion!") she now found it pleasing to rest her head on Harvey's shoulder as she laughed herself into apparent helplessness from what he, not known for his wit, had murmured into her ear. Rick and I watched the display until we grew bored with it. We'd spoken on numerous occasions, of course, but never about anything serious, and never at any length. I'd always assumed he disliked me, the way I assumed, probably wrong-headedly, that anyone interested in sports must dislike me. He was totally devoted to athletics, paying more attention to the smaller man's sports, for his body was beautiful in the way only small athlete's bodies can be beautiful. Much of our contact in the past had come about as he'd approached me for various faculty athletic events, all but one of which I'd declined. It was my one acceptance that he couldn't get out of his mind as we munched our pizza.

"I'll never forget the night you played in the donkey basketball game," he laughed. "Damn you were funny."

"I don't consider slipping off of a stubborn mule into an equally stubborn pile of mule dung particularly amusing."

"And the way you looked when you hit that one basket."

"I did feel triumphant."

"Too bad it was the other team's basket."

"It's the sense of achievement, not the final score that's important."

Rick snorted with delight. "With you on the team, it'd sure have be something other than the final score. You're hopeless."

"Speaking of hopeless, Rick, how's the tennis team shaping up this year?"

"Even you would be an asset. We're considering taking down the nets so our kids might be able to return some shots."

Across from us, Connie let out a whoop of laughter. She'd thrown her arms around Harvey's neck and they were shaking in their seats. Desperation is not pretty. I couldn't imagine what Harvey must be thinking as Connie's red hair engulfed his face like so many licking flames, but Rose, it was apparent, was not pleased. Her face had fallen and her gaze was boring into the pair. But in keeping with her new humanity, she remained silent as Connie and Harvey both came up for air. Rose aimed a glance at me, seemingly imploring me to do something. I shrugged, hoping to tell her that I was not Connie's keeper.

"Aren't you jealous?" Rick whispered.

"Should I be?"

"Aren't you two . . . ? I mean, don't you and Connie . . . ?"

"Go together? Is that the rumor about Connie and me?"

"One of them. Are you saying you two don't date?"

"We're just friends."

Connie let out a noise sure to arouse moose everywhere. This time she succeeded in tipping over her beer. The amber liquid poured into her lap. I expected steam to rise. She excused herself to the restroom to wipe herself off; Rose followed to give aid. Apparently more than aid was offered, for when they returned, Connie was enraged. She picked up her purse and brusquely announced that she was leaving. Staring at Rose she addressed Harvey: "Would you follow me home, Harvey? I've had a little too much to drink and I want someone to make sure I get home safely. Thanks for the lovely evening, Rose. I'll see you all tomorrow. Night."

She circled the table and bent over me, "Be sure to give Mick my regards." Her voice was thick with drink and irony. It seemed that she expected me to be jealous. I gave her a bland smile. She and Harvey, nearly dumbstruck by his good fortune, exited. Bev and Agnes took the opportunity to leave as well. But Rose asked me to stay. Rick, depending on me for a ride home, was forced to stay with me. He ordered another pitcher of beer, and we braced ourselves as Rose stationed herself across from us. Rick nudged me beneath the table. We both expected her to shed her new-found reasonableness and become the Rose of old. However, after only a faint damnation of Connie ("She's spirited, don't you think?") she began to list all the things I could look forward to in this, my tenure year: three unannounced observations by her, one announced observation by Greg Prynne, an appearance before a five-person panel for questioning, and a review of my performance as a teacher. Sometime after Christmas I could expect a decision about my tenure. After that, if I didn't like the decision, I could appeal it to the school board.

"It's really painless," Rick assured me. "I went through it last year."

"With flying colors," she added. "And I'm sure you'll have no problems either, Harper. But beyond our, shall we say, shaky start this year, I have a question. It seems to me that your enthusiasm for teaching has cooled somewhat since you began your career at Arthur. Am I just imagining it, or is something going on that I ought to know about? Do you like teaching any less?"

"Who me?" That was vague enough, I felt. It was a question I couldn't answer when I asked it of myself in private; I certainly wasn't about to start exploring it with Rose. She told me that if at any time I wanted to talk out any problems or discuss the philosophy of teaching, her door was always open.

After a few more minutes of polite but meaningless conversation, we left the pizza parlor. She walked Rick and me to my car, thanking us for making the evening so enjoyable. Rose waved goodbye to us, patted my car door and hurried off to her black car. Rick and I drove on.

"I don't know how you feel about her," Rick said, "But didn't you think Rose was unusually friendly tonight?"

"I thought I was imagining it. Maybe bowling calms her."

A few miles later he surprised me by saying that I should get married.

"Excuse me?" I asked.

"Get married. Get a wife. Have kids. It's a hell of a feeling."

"I don't doubt it."

"I know how you feel. I felt the same before I got married. Who needs it, I said. Everybody does I've decided. To come home at night knowing there's going to be someone waiting for you. Someone to talk to. Or to be quiet with."

"Can't you have that without being married?"

"It's not the same. Not the same at all. Marriage is nice and safe. Cozy, you know. You think I'm crazy. Maybe I am. Maybe its just the afterglow of having the baby but I swear this is the best feeling I've ever known. It's a great cure for loneliness. And in your case it would . . . never mind."

"In my case it would what?"

"Never mind. I talk too much."

"Tell me. In my case, marriage would what?"

"Scotch the rumors."

"More rumors? Good lord, I'm certainly the subject of intense speculation. What's this rumor about?"

"That you don't like women."

"I'm sure you're putting it kindly."

"A little."

"So there are rumors that I sleep with Connie and that I don't like women. Doesn't say much for Connie, does it?"

"Just forget I brought it up. I shouldn't have mentioned it. But remember what I said about getting married. It feels awful good."

When we reached his house a window glowed with orange light. I must admit it looked inviting. "Good night, Harper," he said. "Thanks for the ride. I'm glad we got to talk. You're a good guy."

"So are you. Good night, Rick."

He extended a hand. Looking me right in the eye, he shook my hand, long and firm but still gentle. Then he smiled before going in to his wife and baby. In its way, it was one of the most intimate moments I'd ever experienced.

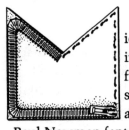ick was not nearly as independent as I'd imagined. In my reveries he dashed about from city to city (drinking martinis from a silver shaker while wearing a tux he'd apparently borrowed from one of my old Paul Newman fantasies), his Lear jet, a hi-tech version of Antony's barge — just as fine as Cleopatra's, though history doesn't note it — waiting to glide him off to another adventure, coming and going as he pleased.

Wrong.

By the second week after our date I was seeing him less as a dashing Prince than as a total stranger. Who was this man I gave my students surprise quizzes for, so I could sit staring out of a window and think of? I didn't know him, not really. My acquaintance with him consisted of one meal and sex on top of a table. What little I knew of him was not particularly good. In college he'd hurt me by refusing to get to know me, and soon it appeared that history was going to repeat itself. I found myself waiting anxiously as if for a long overdue parade, and I grew more impatient with each non-appearance of the grand marshal. Three times in those two weeks Mick called to say that his trip back to see me was on; he gave arrival times and a tentative itinerary of what we would do if we ever got out of bed. Three times he called at the last minute to say "Business" and to cancel our plans. I was angry and hurt and by the third cancellation I told him that if he really didn't want to see me again he didn't have to, but to give his travel agent a break and tell me if he was never going to come back.

"Don't you think I mind having to postpone our plans again?" he asked.

"I like to think so."

"And why am I the only one who can do the visiting? Why don't you come to Chicago?"

He had me there. Why hadn't I thought of that? I asked when I could come. "When do you want to?"

"Right now. I'm tired of it here. I need a break."

"How about next weekend? Is that soon enough?"

"This weekend would be better, don't you think? Friday's the day after tomorrow. I could take a day off and be there Friday by noon."

"This weekend's not good. Next weekend?"

"It's set." And it seemed to be. I'd take both a Friday and a Monday off and make a vacation of it. Mick even suggested that I take a train; I agreed that it might be fun. I was swept along ahead of a wave of details and it wasn't until I hung up that I had my misgivings. Should I go? What would happen? Would I be disappointed again? I paced through the apartment asking my reflection probing questions in various mirrors along the way. He refused to give me any answers until he was framed in a full-length mirror. "Go and shut up about it," he said in that harsh tone he can have at times. "God knows you could stand a change in your life, if only temporary. You like Chicago. Bright lights. Tall buildings. And in this case, sex. God knows you could stand some of that too. Don't be a fool and worry yourself out of the trip. It may be safer at home for you, but it's a lot more boring for me. Don't bother yourself with it. I'll make all the arrangements. You just go off to the bar now."

"I don't want to go to the bar."

"Yes you do. And call Garrick. You haven't done anything with him for awhile."

"Are you going with us?" I asked.

"I'll meet you there."

Wednesday nights at Pay Days were drag and talent night, sometimes not mutually exclusive, which helped draw a reasonable crowd. The feeling was much more relaxed, as if sex in the middle of the week was something to be accepted only under extraordinary circumstances. The patrons of Wednesday nights just wanted to relax and chat with friends while female illusionists and an occasional fire juggler gave them something to chat about. By the time I located Garrick under a palm tree, the show had already begun, the dance floor serving as a stage. Our conversation was limited to a running commentary on the performances. Glitter and boas, skirts slit to the thigh, impersonations of famous females, the acts were more entertaining than outrageous, with more imperfections than polish. It was the flaws, though, that I found most charming. A wig that slipped, false nails that sliced the air on their way to the floor, miscues and miscalculations, these were the moments that made the show worthy of interest and affection.

I was glad that the spectacle interrupted in-depth conversation. Garrick and I had enjoyed little contact in the last weeks. The friendship that had threatened to flourish had never appeared. He was wrapped up in his unnamed lover, to whom he seemed totally devoted though at times visibly vexed by. I had greeted his relationship with glee at his good fortune, but his refusal to reveal any information about his lover had insulted me and I'd withdrawn from him. Further distractions from Mick had left little room for contact with Garrick outside of school, where we spoke but never about anything important, just about teaching. It was as if Rose had gotten her wish that I leave him alone, but for none of her reasons. I felt cheated of a nice friendship.

Garrick must have too. He told me that he'd missed me in his life.

"I wasn't sure if you'd noticed I was gone," I replied.

"I didn't mean to ignore you."

"I haven't felt ignored. Well, just a little."

"I just want to spend all my free time with you know who."

"No, I don't know who. And that's what's hurting my feelings. Why don't you trust me?"

"It's not that I don't trust you. I'm just afraid of what you'll think."

"What I'm thinking now isn't too complimentary."

"I don't want you to hate me. Or him."

"I promise. Please tell me. I don't think we can really be friends until you do."

Connie muscled her way between us. "What are you doing here?" she cried. "Why didn't you invite me?"

"I didn't think you liked this sort of thing."

"I don't."

"Then what are you doing here?"

"I followed you in my car." I thought she was kidding, so I laughed. The slap she delivered across my face let me know she was serious. The noise of her hand clobbering me was covered up by applause as a Jayne Mansfield impersonator eased onto stage. Still, several people around us alternately laughed and gasped as I rubbed my stinging cheeck. "What did you do that for?" I demanded.

"I'm sick of you."

"Apparently. One more trick like that and you're going to be a lot more than sick. Don't you think we'd better talk before one of us gets injured?"

She glared at Garrick. "Get rid of him first."

"Him has a name," Garrick snapped back. "And I didn't do anything to make you mad."

"You can ask him to go for a couple of minutes," I added, "But he doesn't take orders."

She didn't say a word, but continued glaring at him. Garrick slipped away, mumbling something about getting another drink. Her hair looked particularly wild that evening, and even amid all the drinkers I knew from her breath that she'd had several too many.

"You're drunk," I said.

"And you're a bastard."

"Did you really follow me here?"

"I did. I'm sick of being ignored. You used to spend all of your free time with me."

"You used to be fun to spend my free time with. You're not anymore. I'm just as sorry as you are. But until I enjoy your company again, I don't see any reason to submit myself to it."

"It's Mick, isn't it?"

"He's part of it. Most of it is you. You don't own me, Connie. You don't tell me what to do."

"Somebody's got to."

"It's a wonder you can stand being around me if I'm such a weak personality. It probably says something about your many flaws."

She wound up to swat me again. I intercepted her wrist and gripped it painfully until she cried out. People around us told us to be quiet. Connie, ever a crowdpleaser, flipped them the bird. "All right, let me go," she hissed. "You have to make a decision. Right now. Me or Mick. You choose. You can't have us both. If you choose him, I walk out of your life. I'm here. He's hundreds of miles away. You know me. He's a stranger. Which of us is it going to be?"

"I'm not going to make any ridiculous choices like that."

"You have to, you bastard, because I'm telling you to."

"If you insist. I choose Mick. People who really cared about me wouldn't make me choose."

She slapped me hard across the face; I reciprocated with equal strength. She screamed and fell to the floor, lying there, sobbing hysterically. On stage, Jayne Mansfield interrupted her number to see what was going on. She ordered a spotlight be placed on us. Dutifully, a beam crossed the room and illuminated first me, then Connie, on the floor in a large pile.

"What's going on out there?" Jayne asked.

"He hit her," someone cried. The spotlight swiveled back onto me. I hung my head in embarrassment. "Creep," Jayne spat out.

"She hit him first," I heard Garrick call. "Twice."

"Then she deserved it," Jayne said. "Besides, she's bigger than he is." The spotlight now showed Connie in all of her heaving bulk. I felt very sorry for her, but Jayne was right — she deserved it, at least in part. Jayne called the spotlight back to her, told us to keep our mouths shut, and if we had to fight, to do it in the streets. She sang her song again. Connie hauled herself to her feet amid a spattering of applause. She limply gathered her dignity — or what was left of it — around her and headed for the exit. Everything in me wanted to run after her and apologize. Yet I didn't; some things had to be done. Ending my friendship with Connie seemed to be one of them. Maybe that meant a new beginning. I thought briefly of Mick. I found Garrick and hugged him, telling him I wanted to go home. I left, wearily descending the mirrored stairs, noticing only near the bottom that my reflection had something to say. "You're well rid of her as far as I'm concerned," he said. "We've put too much into the friendship and gotten too little out of it. You should be glad this finally happened."

"Then why do I feel so miserable?"

"Probably a chemical imbalance. And you don't listen to me enough."

"And what are you saying now?"

"Don't wait until next weekend to see Mick. Go tonight. Or this weekend at the very latest."

"But he's not expecting me."

"Men like Mick love the unexpected."

I told my reflection to leave me alone. The evening had been hard enough without having to listen to more of his advice. "Think about it," he said just before I reached the last stair and lost sight of him. The cool air outdoors did nothing to calm me. When the first breeze passed over my sweaty face, too cool to be anything but a wind full of approaching winter, I thought briefly of getting in my car and driving straight to Chicago. Then I changed my mind, felt for my keys and started to cry.

Connie called in sick the next day, saving me from a probable wrestling match in the English corridor. But I was depressed all day. Arguments and big changes in my life always left me depressed. The end of my friendship with Connie had involved both. I was very low.

I was about to duck into my third period class a few minutes ahead of the bell. From the hall I heard the sounds of mayhem rolling out of my room. Thinking there might still be time to prevent casualties, I hurried toward my door. A hand, liverspotted yet firm, grabbed my shoulder and spun me around. The hand belonged to Rose. She was wearing a red dress so bright and garish that I nearly shielded my eyes. It came equipped with, of all things, a little cape, a scalloped number the likes of which I hadn't seen since my older sister's

Barbie doll last attended the opera with Ken. "It's time," she said somberly, squeezing my shoulder and gazing meaningfully into my eyes. I felt like Susan Hayward in *I Want to Live*. Soon I'd hear the pellet hit the floor and then things would go black.

"Time for what?" I asked. "If you're talking about the noise in my room, I'm on my way to begin negotiations. I doubt that they've taken hostages yet."

"I'm not talking about the noise. I'm used to that coming from your room. What did you once call it? Primal education, I believe. No, Harper, it's time to be observed. Surprise."

If Susan Hayward had been forced to put up with Rose, she wouldn't have wanted to live.

"Now don't mind me," she continued. "I'll just sit in the back and take prodigious notes." She adjusted her cape, pressed her clipboard to her bosom and strode into my classroom; I followed close behind her. Twenty-seven teenagers immediately fell silent as Rose barreled into view, her miniature cape flapping softly in her wake. They were either awed by the sight of two bona fide Authority Figures (doubtful) or stunned by Rose's outfit. All of them froze in a tableau of disruption: a half dozen boys held yet another high in the air as if offering him as an hors d'ouevre to Ra; several students surrounded a girl who'd had her hair detonated into an au courant style not unlike an atomic explosion; other kids were scattered about the room opening windows, closing drapes, removing items from the bulletin board, searching the contents of someone's purse now lying on the floor. Only a few students remained in their seats. They looked out of place in the chaos. Theresa Laugermann was one of those still seated. She flipped through a book, laughing, as Dean Hopkins peered over her shoulder.

"You have ten seconds to get in your seats or I release the tear gas," I called, sparking immediate laughter and activity.

They rushed to their seats, abandoning the windows and drapes, haphazardly gouging tacks back into bulletin boards, dropping the sacrificial boy, whose head landed on the discarded purse and saved him from certain injury.

Rose was trying to get to a seat in the back row when the tide turned. The kids nearly knocked her down, leaving her gasping and grasping at a desk to keep her balance. From her position in the middle of the aisle she began taking notes. She finished scribbling, underlined something twice and took her seat in the last row. The bell rang and I started class.

"You looked like the crowd scene from *Day of the Locust*," I said. "But you don't understand that, do you? I need an older crowd. Let's get started. Your waiter will be around to your tables soon to take your orders. Drink up and I hope you enjoy the show." Rose looked up with a creased brow and her eyes narrowed. First I took attendance, then I announced a surprise spelling and comma quiz. Rose fairly beamed: "When in doubt, quiz them," was one of her many mottos. Kids who'd brought books whipped them out. Those who didn't have them were full of questions.

"What's a comma look like?" someone asked.

"Like sperm!" someone else replied.

"Then lots of your sentences have potency problems," I replied. Only Theresa and Dean, who laughed, and Rose, who frowned, understood me.

As the kids leaned over their quizzes, tongues exposed as if the answers were written there, Rose motioned me to join her in the back of the room.

"How am I doing?" I asked.

"I'm not at liberty to discuss it right now though I wish I could. Right now I think you'd better get up to the second row. That chubby boy is exposing himself to the blonde who looks like she's drugged."

"She probably is. That's Liz."

I made my way to the second row where chubby Larry was not, in fact, revealing himself to Liz, who seemed more heavily sedated than usual. Rose's mistake, however, was understandable. There was a long rubber snake protruding from Larry's open fly. I tapped him on the shoulder. "Get that snake out of there before I beat your asp."

Satisfied that I'd gotten through to him, I began my journey back to my desk, only to hear gasps and giggles from the class. I turned around in time to dodge the contents of Larry's oversized nose, which, he decided, in retaliation for my being such a killjoy about the snake, belonged on my person more than inside his nostrils. The viscous glop landed with a splat at my feet. From thirty feet away I could hear Rose's head snap up.

"Out!" I shouted louder than I'd ever shouted at a student, or anyone, before. "Get your butt and your nose and your snake out of here and get down to Mr. Prynne's office. You had better be down there when I get there or a tragically early death is a real possibility. Are you going to move any time soon, Larry? You've been canned. But first, clean up your mess."

"I don't have a handkerchief. I'll have to use my hand."

"Good."

Larry wiped up the goop with a trembling hand, then left. Many of the less rowdy students looked frightened that I might turn my ire on them. Others looked disappointed that I was capable of such a reaction, one they'd expect from other teachers but not from me. Theresa and Dean looked embarrassed for me. Perhaps the most ghastly reaction was Rose's, who, having ceased writing, flashed an "okay" sign at me as she beamed her approval.

I quickly wrapped up the quiz and attempted to undo whatever damage I might have done to class morale. It was the first day of our creative writing unit — a unit Rose had protested because, she said, "it might give them ideas." I'd asked the kids to each bring in a book they thought represented good writing. They'd be asked to read one or two paragraphs, then explain what about it they thought was good. Simple though it was, the lesson still fell apart. All but six kids failed to bring in a book. Two of those brought the Bible, another clutched at Webster's Third International and read from page 442, lox to lynx. Another girl read from a medical dictionary. Miguel introduced us to the Spanish translation of *The Hobbit*.

In the back of the room, Rose lapped up the spreading disaster like spilled cream. I called on Theresa Laugermann. Her head was buried in her folded arms. The corner of a thin paperback peeked out from beneath one elbow.

"Theresa," I said hopefully, "Why don't you read now."

She lifted her head high enough to expose one eye, its pupil dilated. "Do I have to?""

"You have a book, don't you?"

"Kind of. I didn't know we were going to have to read out loud."

"Read, Theresa. Open your book, open your mouth and read."

She looked for help from Dean sitting next to her; he rolled his eyes up into his cute little head. She opened the book and mumbled something that would have been inaudible to the most sensitive dog. I asked her to read it again. It was on her third attempt that we heard what she was reading:

"'The door swung open. It banged into the bedroom wall. A square of light fell on Nathan as he lay on the bed. A shadow, dark and burly, blotted out much of the light. On the bed Nathan thrashed about trying to loosen the ropes.'" Theresa hesitated. I urged her to continue, louder so everyone could hear about Nathan. "'"I'm gonna whup you, boy," the burly shadow rumbled. "I'm gonna whup you good." The keys dangling from his belt jangled ominously. Spread-eagle on the bed Nathan watched as the shadow became a man with dark hair and shining sweat. He stood over Nathan uncoiling a long, long whip. "You ready to be whupped good, boy?" He yanked the gag from Nathan's mouth. Naked Nathan moaned with pleasure. "If you whup me it can only be good," he sighed.'"

The good news first: Rose nearly died from the shock. She sucked in all of the available air around her and still she seemed ready to topple from her perch. Her mouth did not quite contain her drooping tongue, and her face turned as red as her little cape.

All the rest of the news was bad: she survived her initial shock and, pulling her tongue back into her mouth, she leaped from her seat, beating me in the race to reach Theresa. She grabbed the book, checked the cover and gasped the title, "*Leather Chaps!*" She clutched Theresa's arm and dragged her toward the door. I grabbed her other arm and pulled, trying to free her from Rose. "Where are you going with my student, Mrs. McCormack?"

"To Mr. Prynne's office where she will be dealt with."

"Don't you think I should handle it?"

"I'm not convinced you can. If you were at all prepared to be a teacher you never would have this silly unit in the first place. We are going back to basics here at Arthur, but not as basic as pornography." She opened the book with her free hand and read aloud, "'Nathan and Marty calmed the pony. While Nathan fed it a carrot up front, Marty walked behind it and . . .'" With a herculean yank, she took complete possession of Theresa and yanked her toward the door. We'd both forgotten that there was a class full of students around us. I rushed across the room and recaptured Theresa's free arm, giving it a pretty healthy yank of its own. Her head snapped back and her hair swished like high grass in a summer storm.

"Class isn't over yet," I said.

"For this one it is. If I have anything to do with it, the semester, the whole year is over for her."

She pulled on her end, I pulled on mine, each ensuing tug more savage than the last. Soon we were pulling simultaneously, nearly rending Theresa asunder. She screamed out in pain. As Rose hesitated, I pulled Theresa to me, encircling her with a protective arm. "Mrs. McCormack," I bellowed, "You're interrupting my class. If there is any punishing to be done, I'll do it. After class. Please leave now."

A smouldering Rose is not nearly as poetic as it sounds. She was so angry her cape was flapping behind her of its own accord. "We'll see about this!" she cried before storming from the room.

"And who says school isn't interesting?" I asked the class.

Rose was back before I knew it, with Greg in tow. They called Theresa and me from the room and ordered us down to the office. Theresa, her head bowed, began to shuffle down the hall, but I refused to move. "I'm not going anywhere," I said, "And neither is Theresa." The latter stopped and looked at me amazed, but, I thought, a little proud. "I'm not one of the kids. I teach here, remember? If you want to talk to me you can do it after class. Come back in, Theresa."

Prynne rumbled. Rose said that Theresa's father had already been called and was on his way to the school. Again they told me to go down to the office. "You're in trouble, King," Greg said.

"I'm not going to your office."

"You're not going back to class."

"Then I might as well go home. See you around." I stalked down the hall. They all watched me; I could feel their eyes on my back. I turned to look at them. "And one more thing. I won't be in tomorrow. I'm going to visit a friend in Chicago."

"King," Greg shouted after me.

"Harper," Rose said, "I can't promise what this will do to your tenure."

I ignored them. Instead I asked Theresa if she wanted to leave with me. She said she'd better stay. Her father was going to be mad enough without her disappearing.

"You want me to stay and talk to him?" I asked.

"There's no talking to him."

I headed up the stairs. "See you tomorrow, King," Greg cried.

"No you won't."

And with that, I left Chester A. Arthur Junior High School — though not quite forever.

The next morning, Friday, I was bright and early at the train station, nearly deserted though this was its business peak for the day. The one train to Chicago would be rolling in soon. Queuing up with a small band of female shoppers, their over-stuffed purses slung by long straps over their shoulders, I considered calling Mick to tell him I was going to visit a week early. But fate had other plans for me and I decided against phoning him. Why not do something totally surprising for once in my life? Stalking out of school had been pretty surprising in itself; all the previous evening I had expected the consequences to call me up on the phone or break down my door. There was only silence. I couldn't help, amid all my turbulent reactions, to feel a little proud of myself. And a little ashamed for leaving Theresa to fend for herself. All in all maybe I was a pretty terrible teacher. But, all in all, maybe it didn't matter any more; maybe I no longer had a job.

In the early morning air, I imagined my coming adventure: I'd slip aboard the train, sleek and silver and leaning forward as if in anticipation of future high speeds. Familiar landscape would be slipped from beneath me like a tablecloth whipped from beneath a dinner for two. Once in Chicago, I'd call his office. Overjoyed, he'd pick me up in a company car and whisk me atop some lakeside tower where he'd fete me with champagne and a view.

My fantasies were interrupted by the arrival of the train. Badly in need of scrubbing down, it limped and wheezed up to the platform. I boarded the weary thing and waited twenty minutes until someone figured out how to make it go again. During the five hour trip (it takes barely four by car) we stopped numerous times, once, I believe, at a fast food restaurant. Wasn't that the engineer I saw talking into a clown's mouth?

We eased into Union Station at the height of the lunch hour clamor. It looked like the halls of Arthur between periods, except there was less acne. About an hour out of town it had started raining. I hadn't brought along an umbrella. Hoping that Mick would be able to pick me up at the station, I walked down the long rain-slickened platform and to a phone booth. I dialed his work number (I'd memorized it before leaving home), but the line was busy. I tried several more times in the next few minutes, but it was always busy.

I decided to take a cab to his office. I found idling by the sidewalk a veritable parade of cabs, bright bumblebees waiting in line at the hive. Hustling through the rain to the nearest cab, I tossed my suitcase in ahead of me, following it with a relieved sigh. That was followed by a gasp as I found myself sitting next to an elderly woman who now had my suitcase in her lap. The driver turned around to look at us. "This is your husband?" he asked her.

"Not that I recall."

I slipped out of the cab and, after a few more false starts, found an empty one. Soaking wet but feeling very cosmopolitan, I hopped in, enjoying the feeling of being chauffeured into the big city traffic. "Where to?" the driver asked.

I realized I had no idea where Mick's office was. I'd memorized his phone but not his address. I asked the driver if he knew where Rising Star, Inc. had its offices.

"I'm not in the mood for riddles. Where to?"

"The John Hancock Building." It was the first place I could think of that would surely have a telephone. I found one at the foot of the monster, looking in the gloom like something from Stonehenge striken with a glandular condition. When I made my call, I didn't find Mick in. "Do you know when he'll be back?" I asked.

"Couldn't even guess. But he'll be in. He has a five o'clock appointment. Want to leave a message?"

I said I'd call back. I went to the top floor of the building, shrouded in clouds (both the tower and my spirits), where I sat on my suitcase and stared out the windows though I saw nothing but white. I was completely discouraged at last. The only bright spot I could discern from the trip so far was that at least I wasn't spending the day at Arthur.

In the clouds I tried to reach Mick again. He still wasn't there. I decided to leave a message. "Tell him Harper King called."

"The comedian from Detroit?"

I went to the Art Institute where I spent two happy hours totally agog. By then it was nearing five o'clock. My feet hurt and the rain had stopped. Looking up the address first, I hopped into a cab and went to Mick's office. It didn't live up to my expectations. Instead of a soaring steel and glass structure, it was located in a squat gray slab of a building on a street I wouldn't want to call home. The office itself was smallish but neat, looking more like a travel agency or a branch of the IRS than anything that had to do with entertainment. A man in a green coat sweater was sitting on the edge of a desk, munching on a swiss cheese sandwich. "Yeah?" he asked between bites.

"I'm Harper King."

"I thought you were black."

"Is Mick here yet?"

"He won't be back until Monday. He changed his plans. His appointment got switched to the other guy's place."

"But you told him I called?"

"Oops."

"Now what am I supposed to do? I just got into town and I was planning on staying with Mick."

"What about his roommate?"

"What roommate?"

"The dancer. What's his name? Jamie."

He jotted an address on the back of a card and told me it was Mick's apartment. "Jamie will take care of you until Mick gets home. He's a good guy." He shook his head as I went to the door. "I saw you on Merv one night," he said. "I could have sworn you were black."

I hailed yet another cab and made my way to Mick's apartment. As I was deposited outside a glass highrise, the sun broke through the clouds just in time for it to begin to set. Rainbows appeared, not in the sky, but on the pavement, where puddles shone like sequins. A doorman wouldn't let me go up to the fourteenth floor. Instead he announced me, speaking briefly on a white phone. "Says he doesn't recognize the name. But he's coming down to take a look at you anyway."

Why hadn't Mick told me about a roommate, I wondered as I settled myself on a bench surrounded by plants with leaves like large green paws. In all of his talk of Chicago, never once had he mentioned that he shared his home with anyone. All sorts of reasons for his silence, few of them good, came to mind as I waited anxiously amid the foliage. An elevator across the lobby opened. A tall, sandy-haired man several years younger than me, with squared shoulders and powerful arms, walked gracefully toward me. This had to be the dancer.

"Harper King?" he asked.

"Jamie? I'm Mick's friend from — "

"I know. I remembered in the elevator who you were. Mick told me about you. Aren't you a week early?"

"After suffering a very bad week, I moved it up some. I thought I'd surprise Mick."

"Mick's never been a connoisseur of surprises. Maybe this one won't be fatal. Next weekend I'll be out of the city so you'd have the whole apartment to yourselves. Here, let me help you with your stuff."

"I hope I'm not intruding. I'll just sit quietly in some corner and won't bother you a bit."

"You'll do no such thing. You're going to keep me company."

In a mirror across the lobby, my reflection winked at me in that leering way it has. It obviously wanted to keep close company with the attractive Jamie.

One side of the apartment was made of glass. The view was of the lakeshore. Two mammoth structures dominated the skyline, like watchful parents guarding their children before allowing them to dive into the blue water. We stowed my luggage in Mick's bedroom (I was glad to see that Jamie had a room of his own) and, equipped with drinks, we sat in the living room watching dusk descend on the city, lights clicking on in the buildings as they clicked off in the sky.

"Do you have any idea where Mick is?" I asked.

"He could be anywhere. His business is unpredictable." He looked off in the distance, rubbing his bare and well-developed arms with thick fingers, though it seemed he did it unconsciously. "He tells me you're a teacher. You like it?"

"Not much. The guy at Mick's office said you're a dancer."

"I was a dancer. I studied ballet until I was seventeen. By then I knew I was too old to go very far. So I danced in bars in New York until a year ago or so ago. I danced here awhile too."

"Now what do you do?"

"You easily shocked?"

"Not that I know of."

"I date professionally."

"You're a hustler?"

"My clientele is exclusive enough that I can call myself an escort."

"And Mick . . . "

"Don't worry. He isn't paying me to live here. He met me when I danced. He loved me there for awhile. Not anymore, though. He brought me with him from New York. Then we broke up but we made pretty good roommates. He doesn't exactly approve wholeheartedly of what I do now, but it pays the rent, so what can he say?"

We talked for an hour. Jamie seemed willing to tell me everything and anything about himself. It was as if he never spoke to anyone. My questions brought a deluge of response. I liked him a lot.

"Why didn't Mick tell me about you?"

"Good question. He can be pretty mysterious sometimes. But you probably know that."

"I hardly know him at all."

"He's a strange one. It's hard second-guessing him. But I love him. You do too I think. It's in your eyes. And he likes you a lot. Maybe he was afraid you wouldn't come visit if you knew he had a roommate."

The phone rang, interrupting us. I hoped it was Mick, but it wasn't. Jamie spoke sweetly to someone on the other end. "But I can't tonight, Georgie. I'll call you tomorrow." He rolled his eyes at me as he hung up. "He's into the father/son trip."

"You broke a date because of me?"

"Of course because of you. I'm going to make you dinner. George needs to be rejected now and then. It makes him that much more grateful the next time he sees me. Now you go take a shower. You must want to clean up after your trip. I'll get dinner started."

I did as I was told. Showering, I was surprised when the curtain was yanked back and Jamie handed me a martini. Only slightly embarrassed, I accepted. We clinked glasses and drank. He looked at my body then ran his fingers across my chest. "No wonder Mick likes you," he said. "We eat in twenty minutes."

The meal was served on a balcony overlooking the skyline. It was really too cool and damp to dine outside but Jamie knew I liked the sight of the big buildings. In my excitement I dropped my wine glass off the balcony; luckily no one was injured.

He wouldn't let me help him clear the table but I followed him back and forth through the apartment to the kitchen. The phone rang again, and again it wasn't Mick. "This is the time of night they start calling," Jamie said. "Want to go out with me and escape them?"

"Won't we miss Mick?"

"Mick's work is a lot like mine. Uneven hours with uneven people. We won't be late. Besides, he's made you wait all day. Shouldn't he have to wait a little too?"

We drove down broad streets lined with towers speckled by light. Traffic was heavy and several cars honked at me as I stuck my head out the window to get a better view. I was taken to an active neighborhood clotted with people and cars. We went to one, two, three bars, each larger and more crowded than Pay Days even on its busiest nights. The men there seemed harder somehow, more determined to be solidly gay. Many were beautiful, others frightening. They were all exciting to me. The third bar had elevated cages, like leftovers from go-go days, in which the most gorgeous men I'd ever seen danced provocatively in g-strings or bikini briefs. The music was nearly visible as it wrapped around their bare bodies, bumping and grinding and egging on the crowd. Several people reached out, trying to tear away the last shreds of garments clinging to the dancers, who moved close, as if they wanted to be stripped too, then moved away before the grasping fingers could do their work.

"You like?" Jamie asked.

"Don't you?"

"I'm a little jaded. I danced here for a few months. Jamie Malone, stripper extraordinaire."

"I'd like to have seen that."

"It can be arranged." He kissed me, as I had hoped he would for over an hour, though I chided myself for wanting such conduct from Mick's roommate. Remembering that I was in town to make love to Mick, not Jamie, I pulled away — perhaps too roughly. "What is it?" he asked.

"Mick."

"He's here?"

"I came to Chicago because of him. I shouldn't be doing this with you."

"Don't you like me, Harper?"

"I like you a lot. More than I should." I let him kiss me again. Then I told him he'd better take me home.

The ride was full of uncomfortable silence. I was embarrassed. Someone less naive in the ways of big city life, I was sure, would have had Jamie then gone home and had Mick with no second thoughts, only second helpings. As we pulled into the parking lot, Jamie grabbed hold of my arm. "If things don't work out with you and Mick, remember me. I have sex with whoever pays me. I love whoever I want."

He unlocked the door to the apartment and said he'd make us coffee. I excused myself to the bathroom, where, I knew, my reflection would tell me off. But I never made it that far. As I passed Mick's room, I heard a noise, as if someone was speaking. At last he was home, I thought. I threw open the door and immediately wished that I hadn't. Mick was, indeed, there. He wasn't alone. They were in bed, Mick riding on top, the other clinging to him from below, clutching Mick's shoulders as he gasped, his legs wrapped around Mick's waist. His heels pushed hard on Mick's ass (still downed with dark curls, I noticed) as they fucked. The one being ridden saw me first. He smiled and waved. "We have company, Mick," he said.

Mick looked over at me, and, to his credit, looked appropriately horrified. He said my name. I fled before we got to formal introductions. I pushed past Jamie who stood in the hall carrying mugs of steaming coffee. An elevator ride, followed by one in a cab, found me at the train station, where this awful day had started. Two hours later I was on my way home, the home I hated but felt safe in, my luggage and hope of a future with Mick left behind me. In front of me, depression, shame and anger lay waiting. My reflection in the window of the hurtling train looked at me pityingly, but laughed anyway.

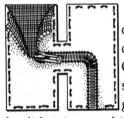ow many times had my feelings about love changed? The figure was starting to mount. Once it had been a religion: I was awe-struck and averted my eyes. Then it was a game: Milton Bradley blew a bundle when he didn't invent this one. Love then seemed a second job with an occasional fringe benefit. Now it had evolved into a combination of all three with a dash of several other more ambiguous feelings thrown in for spice — and a little quiet patch where there were no feelings for love at all, just a bit of numbness, not really unpleasant once you got used to it.

I felt wobbly. It was Saturday night. I hadn't eaten or slept all day. I'd smoked nearly a whole pack of cigarettes since buying them at the train station early that morning. I'd unplugged my phone and paced through my living room most of the day, wrapped in a robe, staring at my reflection as he appeared and disappeared in a mirror across the way. I was confused and exhausted and I told him so. He shrugged and said "What's new?" Taking a sip of the drink he held — I followed his lead — he was surprised when I said "Love is like a piñata."

"Olé."

"I mean it. You stand in the dark and swat at something

that may or may not even be there. Always on the verge of crashing into something. Always about ready to fall on your face."

"But you get all those fun prizes in the end."

"Sometimes that's not enough," I sighed, memories of past loves sweeping over me. "Do you remember loving Franklyn DePalma?"

"You loved him. I just wanted his body. He had a cock the size of Nevada."

"He was as pure as snow."

"Thanks to me you got to put a few tracks in his drifts."

"Then there was my sociology professor, Dr. Haagen. Russell. He said nothing would be different in class if we slept together outside of it."

"He kept his word. We got a C- even though we went down on him the night before the final."

"I'll never forgive him for that. Then there was a string of men, some of them heavenly, some big mistakes, most in between who hung around anywhere from fifteen minutes to two and a half months before wandering off somewhere. Mick was in there too."

"Now there's Mick again," my reflection said, draining his glass. "Should an English teacher be redundant?"

"Is there really Mick again? I pretty well ended that last night when I ran away."

"You fool. You and Jamie should have joined them. Did you see how Mick's ass clenched up when he humped that guy? You never should have let Jamie get away. Who knows the next time you'll be able to have a hustler without paying for him."

"You're talking about sex. I'm talking about love. Sex isn't love."

"Thank god."

There was a sharp knock on the door. I made a face and

my reflection shrugged. There were too many people I didn't want to see. What if it was Mick? I hoped . . . for what I didn't know. I was surprised to find Dean Hopkins from my third period English class looking back at me from the hall. He resembled an oversexed Dennis the Menace. Slouching against the wall opposite my door, his hands were stuffed deep in the back of snug and faded jeans. One leg raised, a knee jutting toward me while his foot jammed flat against the wall. He tossed his shaggy blond hair only partially out of his eyes, looked at me through his bangs and smiled a half-smile. Behind me, my reflection gasped.

"Dean?" I asked. "Is something wrong?"

"Hi, Mr. King. Did I get you out of bed?"

I rearranged the belt of my robe and said I'd been considering taking a shower. Again I asked if there was anything wrong. He said, "Theresa."

"Laugermann? What is it?"

"When her father heard about her reading porn in class he beat her up again and put her on a bus to Minnesota. She jumped off at a rest stop. They don't know where she is."

More bad news; just what I needed to hear. I asked him to come in and tell me everything he knew. It was very little, yet I let him repeat it twice so nice did he look while saying it, all the while sprawled legs apart on my couch.

"That a drink?" he asked. "Can I have one?"

"I don't think so, Dean."

"I've had a really bad day, Mr. King. This thing with Theresa, and I broke up with somebody last night."

"I'm sorry."

"So can I have a drink? It won't be my first."

I relented. At fourteen he probably was more wordly than me. Why the hell shouldn't I supply a minor with liquor? I'd allowed one to be beat up by running away when she needed me. Besides being a failure as a loving person, I was a wreck as a teacher. Returning to the living room with a drink for him and a refill for myself, I found that he'd gone exploring the apartment. He was in the den, flopped in a chair, leafing through a magazine. Spotting the drinks, he grabbed one — mine, the stronger of the two — and wouldn't give it back.

"I shouldn't have left Theresa alone the other day. She couldn't defend herself against all of them."

"I heard you ran out."

"I've been doing a lot of that lately. Sorry to let you and Theresa down."

"You don't have to apologize to me."

"I have to do it to someone."

"You couldn't have done anything to help. Her dad's a crazy man and you know about Prynne and Old Lady McCormack. Besides, the whole thing's really my fault."

"How do you mean?"

"That book Theresa read the other day in class? I gave it to her. It was mine."

"You're gay?"

"I'm everything. You're gay, right?"

"Uh, right."

"Don't worry. I won't tell."

We talked about Theresa morosely, and our tone led us to a conversation about the guy he'd been going with until the night before. I asked him if he went to Arthur.

"I like older men," he said. "But I don't want to talk about it. I'm feeling better just talking to you. Talking about him would only make me sad again."

I asked him what he wanted to do. He held up a large lavender book, my high school annual, and said he wanted to look through it with me. I tried to dissuade him, but he was insistent and we moved to the sofa where we sat side by side. He didn't seem like a kid. As he settled the book on my robed lap, he asked me where I'd gotten such nice legs.

"They just grew there. You don't really want to look at this, do you?"

"For starters. Don't you want me here?"

"I don't want to bore you."

"I wouldn't have come over in the first place if I thought you were going to bore me, Harper. I can call you Harper, can't I?"

"If you want. Tonight. At school, it's still Mr. King."

"Okay Harper. Great name."

I hadn't looked at my yearbook for ages and felt as I leafed through its pages as if I were seeing characters from a television show, long cancelled but cherished in my memory as something special. I found myself telling Dean funny stories about my classmates. His pink tongue danced in and out of sight as he sang out with laughter. Whenever he sipped his drink he'd look at me wide-eyed over the rim of his glass. Soon he had moved quite close, his chin propped on my shoulder, an arm draped around me. I thought of telling him to get away, but I liked the feeling. I felt the rise and fall of his breathing, the beat of his heart against my arm as I continued to chatter about my past. Whenever I stopped my lecture, sometimes just to take a look at him, he'd smile and tell me to go on with my story. When we finally reached my photo, he said I was cute. I tried to deny it, saying he was being much too kind, but he wouldn't allow my disclaimers. He asked if there were any more pictures of me in the book. I turned to one of the gymnastics team.

"You were a gymnast?" he cried, giving me a hug.

"Is that so hard to believe?"

"I didn't mean it that way, Harper. I love gymnasts. I think they're sexy."

He reached in the pocket of his flannel shirt (sleeves rolled up, shirt tail out; with only two buttons buttoned, a portion of smooth torso was revealed to me) and withdrew a fat joint. He put it between his plump lips and lit it.

"What's that?" I asked.

"Surely you've seen a joint before."

"Of course I have. But what are you doing lighting up here?"

"Do you smoke?" he asked as he inhaled. He didn't wait for an answer, passing me the joint. "Take some," he ordered. I did as I was told. I inhaled deeply. The smoke swirled down into my lungs, then up into my head. I felt slightly awash but quite happy. We turned our attention back to the photo of the gymnastics team. I explained that it had been taken when he was four or five years old.

"I'm not four or five anymore." His chin dug deeply into my shoulder as I took another hit. Against my will, the yearbook on my lap rose a notch or two. Dean flicked a finger in the direction of the picture and asked me who the cute boy standing next to me was.

"Franklyn DePalma," I laughed. "I was just thinking about him. He was the first boy I ever . . . " I trailed off.

"The first boy you ever what? Laid?"

"Loved. If haphazardly."

Franklyn had dark hair and dark eyes, short shorts and glasses he was endearingly protective of. We became friends, though tentatively, as if we both longed for more than friendship but couldn't figure out how to go about getting whatever else it was we wanted. It finally happened one day on the couch in the living room of his house. Everyone was gone and we sat side by side, his older brother's *Playboy* between us. Our interest was in a pictorial called "Sex in the Cinema." I focused on the men, usually photographed from behind with their asses in the air as they poised between the waiting legs of some starlet cluttering up the photo. Franklyn's eyes would linger over the more blantantly posed nude men and he seemed reluctant to turn the pages. Our hands touched accidently and we pulled them back as if scalded. I so wanted to touch him again that I did something I then considered brazen: moved my leg an inch or two in his direction, and held my breath while awaiting his reaction. Almost spasmodically, he moved his leg toward. I repeated the movement, and so did he. Finally our knees touched but we pretended not to notice. I was sweating and Franklyn seemed a little short of breath. Though our eyes were directed at the magazine, our vision was glazed by passion. Now it was our hands' turn. His crept toward mine. Mine crept toward his. They touched and our fingers interlaced. We looked in each other's eyes and then attacked. We rolled off the couch onto the floor, buttons flying, shoes skittering across the room, stubborn zippers viciously yanked. By the time our pants were around our ankles I'd learned to kiss with my tongue. I leaned down to put his cock in my mouth but poor Franklyn was so overcome by that time that he ejaculated, scaring the hell out of me and nearly taking out one of my eyes. The sight of him grabbing himself in the throes of orgasm was enough for me. I lay atop him, rubbed against him once or twice and came until I thought I'd done myself permanent damage.

Dean was amused by the story — told to him in a less graphic fashion — not because it was particularly sexy, but because we were content with so little activity. "I hope you got more out of him the next time," he said, depositing the little that was left of the joint in the ashtray.

"There wasn't a next time. We got scared and avoided one another after that. He went to an out-of-state college so I haven't seen him since high school graduation."

"Jesus," Dean whistled. "I bet you get better sex now."

"I have my moments."

"Let's make this one of those moments." He bit my earlobe. I jumped up, my robe falling open for a second. Dean stood too, making no attempt to hide the large ridge in his tight jeans. He locked his hands behind my neck and kissed me, his tongue driving deep into my mouth.

"I'm your teacher for Christ's sake," I gasped, pulling away though not until we had kissed for long, accelerating moments.

"Forget you're my teacher. Other people have." With quick movements he whipped off his shirt, tossing it on the floor. "Do you like my body?" he asked.

"Do you have to ask?"

"I like to hear people say it. Do you think it's nice?"

"It's beautiful." I kissed him, losing my fingers in his shaggy hair.

"Do you want to make love to me?" he asked. "You can. I want you to." He slipped my robe off my shoulders, pushed it down my body and to the floor. "Take me to bed, Harper. Please." When I hesitated he took the lead. I followed him down the hall to the bedroom. He was wearing no belt. A twist and a yank were all it took for his jeans to slip off. Deft moves I could never duplicate allowed him to step out of his jeans, socks and shoes all at the same time. He wore no underwear. He stood naked in front of me. He cupped himself in his hands and whispered, "It could use some loving." I knelt and took him my mouth, feeling him expand and grow hard. Then he pulled me up, gasping my name, leading my kisses back to his waiting mouth. We lay on the bed. He told me to lie on my back while he positioned himself above me. He licked his hand and moistened my cock. With a sharp intake of breath he lowered himself onto me; I moaned as I slid into him. "I want you to fuck me," he whispered, and I did. He came and a few strokes later, driving deep within him, so did I. He lay on top of me, both of us filmed by sweat, and flicked at a nipple with his tongue. "Did you like it?" he asked.

"You ask the silliest questions."

"Tell me. What grade would you give me, teach?"

"An A."

"No A plus?"

"Don't be greedy, Dean."

"I'm greedy. For you." He kissed me, but there was a knock at the door. I groaned and crawled out of bed, grabbing my robe and telling him to stay put and stay quiet. As I got to the front door I heard Dean leave the bedroom and lock himself in the bathroom. A moment later I heard my shower running. A sharp rap rang out and I opened the door. There was Garrick looking just awful.

"Harper?" he asked meekly. "Am I interrupting anything?"

"Uh."

"Is that a yes or a no? I can go away."

"You look miserable. Have you been crying?" His eyes were red-rimmed, pale tracks running down his splotchy cheeks. He sniffed and denied he was crying. Then he burst into tears. I steered him into the apartment and settled him in a chair where I knelt. His head was buried in his hands. When he looked up he asked me why I was wearing a bathrobe so early in the evening. He said he hoped I wasn't sick.

"I was about to take a shower."

"Oh yeah. I can hear the water. What I have to tell you may take awhile. You might want to turn it off."

"That's okay," I stuttered. "I have plenty of water. What's up?" Jesus, I thought, I hope he makes this quick. What would he do if he found out I'd just had sex with a student? He rubbed his temples with the palms of his hands and sighed heavily. Looking at me glumly, he told me he was in trouble. "You were the only person I could think of to tell. Now I'm not sure I can tell you either. I'm afraid to." He started crying again. I asked him if he wanted to blow his nose. "No," he answered proudly as he snuffled and wiped his eyes with a shirt sleeve. "I'm going to tell you about the guy I've been going with."

"The mystery man?"

"I think I'm in love with him."

"But that's wonderful."

"No! That's terrible."

"I don't understand."

"Let me start from the beginning."

The beginning was inelegant. One evening while Garrick was walking aimlessly around a gargantuan mall a mile or so from Arthur (where lonely people frequently walk in order to be near other people), he sought out the nearest restroom, tucked away in the far corner of a large discount store, smelling of caramel corn and cotton candy (the store, not the restroom, which had an aroma all its own). After paying a dime to get in the door, he found himself in a surprisingly large, ill-kempt and ill-lighted room with three stalls painted a nauseating green, and a urinal full of cigarette butts with a pink wafer at its bottom that did nothing to clear the air but did a fine job of clogging the drain. A man leaned against the wall, awaiting relief, apparently, for all of the stalls were occupied. Garrick, too, positioned himself against a wall. He couldn't help but notice that the man beside him stared blatantly at his crotch. After several minutes, a man emerged from the center stall. He seemed to have trouble with his fly, for he was exposed a long time, wrinkled hands fluttering as he searched fruitlessly for the zipper. The man against the wall indicated with a nod that Garrick should take the now-empty stall. He realized that he'd stumbled onto a gay bathroom.

On the seat, he surveyed the plethora of graffiti on the surrounding walls. Illustrations and advertisements for sex for hire or fun decorated every free space, except for two glory holes, about three inches in diameter lovingly constructed by someone (by whom? do people walk around with brace and bits for just such emergencies?) in order to afford himself and others the means by which to have sex without leaving the privacy of the stalls. Garrick felt a combination of emotions: curiosity, amusement and a certain amount of sexual excitement. He was not unaware of such places, having used them as the outlet for his sexual life the first few years of college. He looked at the shoes of those in the stalls on either side of him, trying to ascertain what sort of men squatted nearby. To his left was a pair of mud-spattered work shoes with waffled soles; to his right, a smallish pair of white tennis shoes with three stripes on each side. The tennis shoes promised the most interesting owner. The work shoes, however, made the first move.

After the two men outside the stalls held a whispered conversation and left together, the owner of the work shoes inserted his penis, unspectacularly erect and a dingy gray, into the glory hole in a request for instant gratification. Resisting the temptation to swat the intruder with a mighty backhand, Garrick peeked through the hole on his right. A blue eye stared back at him. Having lost his enthusiasm, as well as his erection, the work shoes pulled up his pants and departed, leaving Garrick and the tennis shoes alone. The latter slipped him a note written on toilet paper. "What's up?" it read. Garrick didn't know how to respond so he sat motionless and didn't write anything. The blue eye returned to the hole and looked at him. As it pulled back, Garrick caught a glimpse of blonde hair and a broad smile. Then, with a slight creaking of joints, the tennis shoes knelt and slipped a beautiful cock beneath the wall. For a moment Garick was mesmerized, then he reached out and grasped it. After a few rocking motions that ran his length in and out of Garrick's surprised but grateful grip, he stood, taking away his offered gift. He passed another note. This one requested that they go somewhere more private and see what would happen. Garrrick nodded at the blue eye. They met outside the stalls. Garrick noticed the boy's youth — he was reminded of his college days which now seemed so far away — and, after a mutual fondling of crotches, they repaired to Garrick's apartment where they put in six hours of boisterous sex before falling asleep, exhausted, in each other's arms.

Garrick hesitated in the telling of his tale. I thought he might cry again. I surely understood his dilemma. "Just because you met in a less than glamorous way doesn't mean your relationship is any less real."

"We don't have a relationship any more. He broke up with me yesterday."

"Garrick, I'm sorry."

"He didn't call me yesterday afternoon after school like he usually did. I got worried and called him. He asked if I'd gotten his note. He'd given it to Mary. It said that he thought I was getting too serious and he wanted to break up. You can imagine how I felt. But I managed to call Mary and ask her if anyone had left a note for me. She said yes, and called him by name. Now that she thought about, she said . . . "

"Let me guess. She put it in Elmo Dobson's mailbox."

"So Elmo has a Dear John letter meant for me and Mary knows who it's from."

"Just go to school early Monday morning and get it out of Elmo's mailbox."

He told me to let him finish his story and then I'd see why he couldn't wait until Monday morning.

Waking up together, they'd made love again and pledged their devotion to one another. It was while they were dressing that his new lover asked Garrick for a ride to school. Garrick asked if he went to City College.

"I don't go to college."

"What high school?" Garrick asked, feeling slightly nervous.

"You really don't know, do you?"

"Know what?"

"I go to Chester A. Arthur Junior High School."

Garrick stopped the recounting of his story when he saw the look of horror that swept across my face. He thought he knew the reason and threw himself at my feet. "Don't hate me!" he cried. "I didn't know. I thought he was a lot older. You've got to help me Harper. You've got to break into the school tonight and get that letter from Elmo's mailbox."

I stared at him as if I were a guppy. I asked him who the student was, though I was loathe to hear the answer. In the bathroom, the water stopped running. Garrick noticed. "How'd it do that?" he asked.

"A timer," I replied. "Tell me, Garrick. Who's the student you're in love with?"

"Dean Hopkins." Now that he'd said it, I wasn't surprised. I didn't fall writhing onto the floor. In fact, I didn't react at all. "You don't seem surprised."

"I had a feeling it was Dean."

"You knew he was gay?"

"I knew he was advanced. I didn't know he was gay until recently."

We heard the bathroom door open and close, then the bedroom door do the same routine. Garrick looked at me confused. "Is someone back there?"

"Uh."

"You have a visitor. Is it Mick?"

"Good guess. But that's all right. We've got to get right over to school and find that note. No time to lose. You warm up the car while I get dressed."

"What about Mick?"

"That lazybones? He'll stay right in bed."

"Can I meet him?"

"Maybe later. No time to lose right now. Hurry up. We have a spying mission to attend to." I practically threw him out of the door, then hurried to my bedroom. Dean, blond hair made brownish by his shower, lay amid tangled sheets, his arms reaching out to me. "Come back to bed, Harper. Let me suck you. Nice and slow and long." When I began dressing he asked me what was wrong.

"Do you know who that was?"

"The Avon Lady."

"Garrick. Why didn't you tell me it was him you were going with?"

"Would you have gone to bed with me if I'd told you about him?"

"I shouldn't have gone to bed with you anyway. You're a kid."

"I'm not a kid."

"Then you're my student. Teachers shouldn't sleep with students."

"I can handle it. Can't you? You've wanted me a long time. I've seen the way you've looked at me. You thought I didn't notice. You wanted me."

"Yes, but ... "

"And I wanted you, Harper." He hopped up and tried to take my shirt off. "Come back to bed. Please. It'll be okay. Look what you've done to me." He was hard again. He moved forward until his cock lay within my hand. I curled my fingers around him, then shouted "No! I can't!" I calmed myself and tried to dress again. "Garrick's waiting for me in the car. The note you gave him got put in the wrong mailbox. He could lose his job. And he's about to lose his mind. We're going to break into the school and get it back."

He sat on the edge of the bed and looked forlorn. "I didn't mean to get him in trouble. First Theresa, now Garrick. I'll be here when you get back Harper. I want to be with you so bad. I get so lonely sometimes."

Dressed and ready to leave, I couldn't stop myself. I rushed to the bed and knelt before him, feeding hungrily between his legs, my hands desperately moving across him. Then I jumped up, so mightily confused that I could barely find the door. It was difficult to look back at him lying there, holding himself, still glistening with my saliva.

"Don't be here when I get back," I said. "Please be gone, okay? But don't leave until your hair dries. I don't want you catching cold."

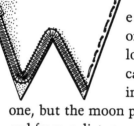

e crept from the car, bent at the waist and on tiptoe. Sneaking through the parking lot, peeping over the hood of an occasional car, crouching by mud-spattered tires. Our impersonation of spies was a bad one, but the moon played its part by dodging behind a cloud, and from a distance we may have looked as if we knew what the hell we were doing. The plan, such as it was, called for entry through the English hall since the keys I had been awarded after two years of stewardship would unlock only the door at that end of the building. If we got in undetected, we'd select the route according to prevailing conditions.

"Thanks for doing this for me," Garrick whispered over my shoulder as we climbed the concrete steps that led to the door.

"I haven't done anything yet." Guilt acted as blinders. On the ride over I'd managed not to look at him. It was possible that I would never look him in the eye again. I was certain that our friendship, the last one I had intact, was only a confession away from being over forever.

I expected an alarm to go off as I unlocked the door, but we were undetected and went in. We felt our way down a flight of stairs until the familiar sticky feeling of the hall's linoleum was beneath our feet. The kids tended to view the English department as a landfill. This staircase was notorious for its unsanitary condition. Students congregated there for their morning cigarette, joint or cocktail. A lingering stench, like a bar around closing, was impossible to dispel. Somewhere in the distance music played. Usually I loved the sound of a radio in the dark of night; it seemed more human then. I loved to drive alone at night, the pink smudge of dawn hours away, moisture hissing beneath my tires, the radio my only companion. Now, however, the music wafting toward us was anything but reassuring. Like a broken twig in the woods, it meant danger ahead.

"Radio," Garrick whispered. "Upstairs."

"I hope it stays there. I didn't know janitors worked on Saturday nights." I pried my foot from the sticky tile. "I wasn't aware that they worked at Arthur at all."

But Garrick wasn't listening. He raised a quaking finger to point down the hall to the door of Rose's office. It was partially open and a yellow bar of light extended nearly halfway across the hall. Someone was in there. Garrick mimed a hair-pulling fit and clung to me in the deepest shadows. As I sank into a crouching positon, my knee gave a resounding crack. We cowered against a wall, waiting for Rose to burst out upon us, in stormtrooper drag and with two attack dogs, under control but just barely, their maws salivating like Niagara. We waited. Nothing happened. We waited some more. My legs developed cramps. Using my fingers as well-manicured albeit uneven legs, I signalled to Garrick that we would go on down the hall past Rose's office. I clamped my hand over his mouth as he began to gasp his disapproval of my plan. After what I had done to him and Dean and a cast of thousands in my life, I didn't care if I did get caught. I shrugged a devil-may-care shrug befitting my leadership role and, doing my best General

MacArthur, waded down the hall knee-deep in darkness, not knowing if I should ever return.

I stopped when I was nearly even with Rose's door. Pressing myself against the wall, I measured up the situation. The door was open about two feet, the same width as the line of light extending into the hall. There was certainly enough non-illuminated area left to facilitate our passage, but still I was unsure. How far into the hall could whoever was in there see? What the hell, I thought? Torture and death would only be two more in a long line of disasters in my life. I took off my shoes, not an easy process when one wants to remain silent. The first shoe slipped off uneventfully, but the second leaped from my hand and it was only after several breathless moments of dextrous juggling that I caught it by a shoe string, just as it was about to crash to the floor. Tucking it safely under my arm, I looked at Garrick — who lay flat on his back. I suspected a massive coronary, but he finally moved. Handsignals — those that weren't obscene — urged me to be more careful.

I tiptoed directly in front of Rose's door, the light at my stockinged feet. I stopped, something a seasoned spy would be loathe to do, but I wanted to know who exactly was in there. A uniformed janitor sat at Rose's desk, her sneakered feet propped on a pile of papers by the phone. She read a paperback romance (*Love's Belching Smokestack*, I think the cover said) and slowly snacked on some foodstuff unrecognizable, apparently pulled from the crumpled white bag at her side. Rose would be livid at this invasion into her territory. One practically had to have written permission even to enter her lair. Suddenly the janitor's head flashed up and the book dropped to her lap. She seemed to be staring directly at me. I was certain that our eyes met as she pushed herself out of her chair. My sweaty palms slid down the wall behind me. I removed them before they emitted an incriminatingly flatulant noise. She crossed the office in three long strides, her face growing more clouded with each. But she didn't race into the hall wielding a dust mop with which to bludgeon me. Instead she opened a drawer in a file cabinet just next to the door and removed her purse, searching frantically within it for something. Then she smiled and pulled out a small box of animal crackers. Returning to the desk, she picked up her book and contentedly read on, inserting first a lion then a giraffe between her moving lips. I moved past the door, weakly signaling Garrick to follow. With much trepidation but no incident he scurried to my side, collapsed in my arms, and, reviving him, I hustled us out of the English hall.

"Why did you go so slow?" he hissed. "James Bond does it a lot quicker."

"I'm a breed of spy all my own."

We worked our way up a little-used flight of stairs, which, musty and dusty, took us backstage of the equally little-used auditorium. A work light encased in a crusty stage shined dimly, revealing pulleys and ropes rising upward only to be swallowed by the darkness a few feet above our heads. Limp curtains — one tan, one black, one red and faded — divided the wooden stage into three parts. Plays were no longer performed here. Neither teachers nor students wanted to put in the time necessary to elevate sheer disaster to mere mediocrity, and the drama club and been forced to put its grease paint into a much needed retirement. The show may go on elsewhere, but not at Chester A. Arthur. Even the band and choir had foregone the auditorium, inexplicably favoring the cavernous gym for their concerts, off-key barrages played to the accompaniment of squeaking bleachers. The auditorium was used for study hall, occasional club meetings, and little else. The stage we wandered about on had been dormant for years, and it showed.

"This is kind of spooky," Garrick whispered, running a hand up and down a thick twisted rope. Dust balls rose in the air. I stuck my head through the red curtain. I could see the first two of dozens of rows of seats upholstered light blue. They stared back at me. "I just love opening nights," I said, withdrawing my head.

"Is Mr. Ziegfeld here?"

"Third row center. Is my makeup on straight?"

"Yes, but your face is crooked."

"There's never a rimshot around when you need one."

"Did you ever want to be an actor?"

"Not really. I didn't want people to see how much I could feel."

He thanked me again, causing a renewed attack of guilt. I wondered if Dean had left my apartment yet. Would he make the bed or leave it to look up at me and make me hurt all over again? Garrick told me he'd made a decision. The announcement interrupted my own thoughts. "I'm going to take my mother up on her offer," he said. "I'm going home and starting law school."

"You're going to quit teaching? When?"

"At the end of the semester, I guess."

"Does this have anything to do with Dean?"

"Some. I think going with him helped me make up my mind."

"Going with him? Or breaking up?"

"Going with. When he told me that morning he went to Arthur I almost fainted. He was a kid. People get arrested for doing what I'd just done. But he didn't seem like a kid and, thanks to teaching, he was the most eligible bachelor I'd run into. Although I loved every minute of loving him, I don't want my life to depend on sleeping with my students for my sexual fun. I have to quit."

"I'll miss you."

"Haven't you ever thought about a student in sexual terms?"

"This isn't the time or the place to discuss it, Garrick."

"I disgust you. You find me beneath contempt."

I plopped down on an abandoned three-legged stool. It tilted and nearly tipped me onto the floor. I toyed with a curtain — the black one — instead of sitting. "Let's just say," I began slowly, nearing a decision, "That you aren't the only one to sleep with a student."

"Really? You?"

"Really. Me."

"When was it? Who was it?"

I reached my decision: I might as well risk the last friendship I had; I'd lost all the rest of them and still I survived. At least I'd always know I'd been honest with him.

"It was tonight."

"Tonight?" Garrick sat on the stool I had abandoned. It didn't tip at all. Even furniture has it in for me, I thought. I could see his mind working.

"I only told you it was Mick because it seemed like the best thing to say at the time. Someone came to my door about an hour before you to there. He'd come to tell me that Theresa Laugermann ran away. One thing led to another and . . . Garrick, this is real hard for me to say."

"Then let me say it for you." He stood and his face was erased by shadows. "It was Dean Hopkins, wasn't it?" I nodded. "He was in the shower while we talked?" I nodded again. "Is that where you did it? In the shower?"

"Garrick."

He exited stage left, up a short flight of stairs and out into the hall. I followed, expecting to find him weeping or storming or waiting to tear out my heart. But he looked triumphant as he paced up and down the hall.

"Garrick?" I asked. "Would you like to kill me now or draw it out so it hurts more?" He actually laughed. "This isn't the response I expected. You're not mad? Or hurt?"

"Sure I am. But not at you. I know what Dean is like. And you're almost as hard up for a man as I am. Sorry, Harper. But it's true, isn't it? Mick's miles and miles away. You can't be expected to hold out forever when someone like Dean throws himself at you. And Dean can throw himself with the best of them. That little bastard. I shouldn't have told him you were gay. It gave him a new challenge. And I should have told you from the very beginning that it was Dean I was involved with. If you'd known it was him, you wouldn't have let him seduce you."

"You really forgive me?"

"There's nothing to forgive. We've both been had by an expert."

"Had in several senses of the word." What a relief I felt, having salvaged at least one friendship.

We proceeded to the Administrative Suite, only once lunging into shadow as once again the radio music rolled toward us, a used car ditty growing louder and more threatening, before disappearing without doing us any harm. We moved on. Not surprisingly, the office door was locked. I thought Garrick would burst into tears as he stared, frustrated to his very limits, at the stubborn door, the last obstacle in our effort to save him. "Let's pick the lock," he said desperately. "Do you have a hairpin?"

"Please."

"Well, do *you* have any suggestions?"

"We could mug the janitor and grab her keys."

"How about something less violent?"

"You could seduce her. While you're having your way with her heaving flesh, I could sneak the keys and — "

"Shut up, Harper."

"Right."

We rattled the knobs of adjacent doors in hopes that one would yield, unlocked. One did. The door to the nurse's office swung open. Past a small white enamel table and a small white enamel wastebasket was a door to a second room where two small white enamel cots squatted in the available light. In that room was a door that led into the Administrative Suite. It, too, was unlocked. Garrick squeezed my hand in triumph and hurried toward the pigeonhole mailbox where he found what he had expected to find. He was about to tear up Dean's letter, but thinking better of it, he handed it to me. I moved near a window and by moonlight — the moon had repositioned itself in order to follow the further adventures of the hapless spies; heavenly bodies need entertainment too — I read the short letter, written in Dean's recognizable hand, round, round o's and a's, and long strokes below the line. The contents were devastating to Garrick but grammatically correct, a small victory for me. We both were silent as we stood in the dim office. As I was thinking of Dean, I was certain that Garrick must be doing just the same. I remembered how Dean had looked when I'd answered the door; how his dimpled navel had winked at me from the strip of his bare stomach; how his chin had dug into my shoulder as we sat side by side on my couch; how, naked, he had fondled himself, asking me to love him as I sank to my knees and let his long softhardness ease into me until I felt my chin come to rest in the silky valley between his oversize balls.

Guiltily, I pulled myself out of my thoughts and told Garrick that we'd better get going, that I'd take him to the bar and we'd have an infinite number of much-deserved drinks. We were retracing our steps through the nurse's office when we heard keys jangling very near the door toward which we were heading. Our comic panic caused the observing moon to shimmer with laughter. We bumped into one another several times before scurrying into Greg Prynne's office, blessedly unlocked, just as the door to the nurse's office turned beneath someone's hand. We dived beneath Greg's desk as we heard footsteps in another part of the office, always drawing nearer. Crouched face to face under the desk, we stared into one another's frightened eyes, the whites now looking like the albumen of eggs in the light of the amused moon.

The door to Greg's office opened. We heard the soft scraping of shoes on carpeting, then, in the distance, Willie Nelson telling anyone who cared to listen that he was on the road again. A radio: that damned janitor again! She apparently had been assigned to guard the building like a music-loving hound of hell. She was everywhere: at this moment at Greg's desk, plopping heavily into his chair, her spread knees within inches of our faces, her crepe-soled orthopedic sneakers tapping in time to the music. We heard her fingers burrow with little clicks into the ever-present bowl of M & M's on Greg's desk. One little candy oval slipped off the desk, rolled down her lap and did a neat ricochet off the bridge of my nose. Luckily, she didn't try to retrieve it — who was she, after all, to clean up messes? — and instead sat placidly chomping on the M & M's while scratching herself in the most embarrassing places. Finally, she pushed away from the desk, crossed the office, shut the door, and left us, relieved and undetected. After a few moments we crawled from beneath the desk, first making sure we still had Dean's letter, and headed for the door and our escape.

Were we really surprised to find that the door was locked from the outside and that we were trapped in Greg Prynne's lair?

I surprised Garrick, however, with my reaction: I laughed. Not the loud guffaws I wanted to emit, but in heaving silent gales, doubling over at the waist, leaning on Greg's desk for support. Garrick, upon realizing that I was not convulsing on top of all our other problems, joined in my silent mirth. We laughed helplessly until we fell into a perspiring, breathless heap on the floor. Several of the papers from Greg's desk floated down with us, sticking to our sweaty skin.

We lay side by side on the floor, laughed out at last, staring upward, where, somewhere in the darkness, there had to be a ceiling. Garrick suddenly snapped his fingers. "The windows," he said."

"Only open halfway. Prevents students from escaping."

He thought another moment. "We could rush the door."

"We couldn't rush a sorority."

"So what are we going to do?"

"Lie here until Monday morning."

"Staring at the ceiling?"

"We could roll over and stare at the carpet if you'd like."

But we got up and moved aimlessly around the office as if hoping for an alternate escape route, as yet unnoticed, created by some Midwestern Ali Baba. None was found. We were forced to sit down and try to get comfortable. Greg's chairs were well-cushioned, at least.

"Do you like what I've done with the place?" I asked, looking around the office. "Of course the house won't really be complete until after the pool is in. But we try. Lord knows we try."

"And your houseboy," Garrick joined in. "My dear, he is one of the loveliest creatures I have ever seen. Wherever did you find him?"

"Through a service. And, I might add . . . " here I dropped to a whisper, " . . . his references are *im* - pressive indeed."

We laughed, and I said it would be fun, wicked but fun, to sully Greg's desk with some steamy sex. I remembered my encounters with Mick all those years ago atop the table, but I didn't mention that to Garrick, who surprised me by asking if I'd liked having sex with Dean.

"Of all the things we have to talk about at this moment, why should we discuss the quality of sex with a minor?" My chiding, however, was not of the stern variety.

"I'll tell if you tell," Garrick said.

"Forget it."

"That good, huh?"

"You should know. And we both should know better. Change the subject please."

And he did immediately: "What do you look for in a man?"

"After tonight, a sixteenth birthday at least."

"No really."

"A sense of humor. A sense of responsibility. A sense of the ridiculous. A pulse rate. That's it. How about you?"

He pondered for a moment. "He has to be a good kisser."

"That's on my list too."

"Are you a good kisser?" Garrick asked. "No, don't answer that. I already know."

"You do?"

"I could tell from the first time I saw you, your lips, that you'd be a great kisser."

I was slightly embarrassed and more than slightly aroused. The moon, stepping out of its passive role of entertained bystander, became a more active participant, changing its light to something much more romantically vibrant; could I really feel the light in my thighs? I steered our conversation elsewhere. I had him fill me in on what had happened at school in my absence on Friday. Rose, it seemed, had huddled in this very office most of the day, devising strategy against me, no doubt. She assigned a student teacher to take over her classes, showing her students an animated filmstrip on the life and times of Carl Sandburg narrated by Orson Welles or Orson Bean or someone, Garrick forgot exactly who.

I explained that Rose used to use only filmstrips narrated by Rod McKuen. "He was her favorite poet. She once told me that Rod spoke to her directly. About a year ago I mentioned that I'd seen Rod on a rerun of the Hollywood Squares, and that he had been the Secret Square. She didn't react at all favorably. She'd heard certain rumors that have given her pause, she said, rumors of an unnatural variety, if you get my drift, she added, raising then drooping an eyebrow, though not as effectively as Greg can. I wanted to tell her that I'd been 'drifting' for years, but didn't. She's had it with Rod, I'm afraid."

"Well, on Friday, she looked more like something out of William Blake than Rod McKuen. You should have seen her. I was in the office getting my mail and Rose was just standing there staring at the clock. When the last bell rang and you still hadn't signed in, she sort of went wild. Her head bounced all over and her hands — well, fists really — jerked around like she was looking for someone to slug. I discreetly slipped into a corner. I swear there was spittle all over her lips. She scared the hell out of me. I think you'd better start looking for a new job, Harper. How about in Chicago? By the way, I haven't even given you a chance to talk about your trip. Weren't you supposed to go there this weekend?"

The sketchiness of my answer told him that things had gone badly. Little by little I told him the whole story.

"Wow," Garrick breathed. "You've had quite a rotten weekend yourself. And it looks like it's just beginning."

"Yeah, but I'm at least a good kisser."

We sat silently looking at one another, a pose we kept for a very long time. Then, still without speaking, we got out of our chairs and, lowering ourselves to our knees, sank to the floor. Our faces inched toward one another and met, at long last, in a kiss. I took him in my arms; he felt somehow even slighter than had Dean a few hours earlier. We lay down on the floor.

Despite the fact that there is something slightly mad about trying to remain in a satisfying kiss while attempting to undress yourself and your partner, that is what we tried. We had to part as I pulled his sweater over his head — a stubborn fuzz ball adhered to his moist lips and we had to wait until that had been plucked — but finally we were unclothed. Naked, Garrick looked a lot like Dean: a well-developed youthful body with a generous cock and heavy pendulous balls. His nipples were taut and tauntingly pink with brownish tones, daring me to take them in my mouth. Never dare a man with an erection. I took one between my lips and sucked hard; it grew even larger under pressure. "Bite it," Garrick whispered fiercely, "Bite it hard. Harder."

Sex is flesh and blood, taste, touch and smell, and any attempt to render it into simple nouns and verbs can never be totally successful or satisfying, not when compared to the real thing. Let's leave it that Garrick's nouns were the real things, and his skill with the verbs was nigh onto remarkable. Whatever I was doing to various parts of his body, he made me apply pressure to his nipples; when my hands were busy elsewhere, he took care of them himself, at times almost savagely pinching them, never harder than when, with a grunt and a sigh, he sent his spongy juices down my throat.

I feared that talking afterward would be difficult. But it wasn't. We took what we had just done for what it had been: something we'd been curious about from the beginning, something we'd wanted to do. It was as if we sensed that our lives were soon to take us in different directions, and we wanted to share this before our journey began.

Soon we were very tired. Our emotional and physical exertions of the past days had left us exhausted. Greg had a couch in his office that might have slept two, but we opted for the floor, where we lay naked, holding one another, not in any erotic way, but rather in a comforting, friendly manner. Garrick fell right to sleep. His body relaxed, became slack, and rolled away from me as his breathing became soft and regular, marked only by the slight rise and fall of a shoulder.

However, I could not sleep so easily. A veritable convention was taking place in my head. A cast, if not of thousands, then substantial, refused to recess, just wouldn't let me alone long enough to rest. Mick, Jamie, Dean, Theresa, Connie, Rose, Greg, and even Garrick were represented in the throng by loud voices hurling their requests and questions and woes at me, none that I could help with or respond to, but none that I could ignore. For twenty bothersome minutes I lay there, further from sleep than when I had put down my head — without even a pillow to plump into submission.

At last the voices became too much. I got up and took Greg's phone into a far corner. I dialed Mick's number in Chicago. Jamie answered.

"Harper!" he cried. "Where are you?"

"You wouldn't believe it. Is Mick there?"

"He's out looking for you."

"Well call him off. I'm back home."

"That's where he is. We were so worried about you that he drove down late this afternoon to try and find you. He has your luggage with him. You left it here when you ran out. Hasn't he come to your apartment yet?"

"I haven't been home for awhile."

"You are home. You aren't home. Where exactly are you?"

I explained as cogently as I could what had happened and where I was; it took awhile before Jamie understood and believed me. Through his laughter, he asked if there were anything he could do to help. Short of calling a locksmith, I said, he could tell Mick to come over to the school and help us if he heard from him before he returned to Chicago.

"He's sorry, you know, about last night," Jamie said.

"Is he?"

"You know he is. He likes you a lot. And so do I. Just remember that. You have two big fans in Chicago. In fact, we've been talking about you all last night and today. We've come up with a plan. Want to hear it? No, I'll let Mick tell you about it."

"Since the chances are good that I'm never going to get out of here, why don't you at least give me a clue as to what you talked about?"

"We want you to move to Chicago and live with us. Now, Harper, don't say anything yet. Just listen to me. Mick says you're not especially happy doing what you're doing. You told me that yourself over dinner last night. He says you're capable of bigger things, exciting things, and I believe him. Remember, kiddo, Mick's a talent scout. It's his job to spot potential."

"Yes, but . . . "

"Quiet. Just listen to me, I said. You could come here and live. We both like you. A lot. We have this huge apartment that has room enough and more for you. We have lots of friends who know lots of people who know how to help you get what you want."

"But the problems, Jamie."

"Of course there would be problems. But we'd help you solve them. There'd be lots of things to figure out, but the most important thing is that you decide to do this, to make this big step. Once you do that, the problems will be secondary. They'll take care of themselves. What are the alternatives? Continue exactly as you are now? Think about it, kiddo. We want you. You want change whether you'll admit it or not, and we can give you that. In spades. And we like your body."

"This is all very sweet, but — "

"Think about it. I don't believe you'll disappoint us. Or yourself."

With that, we hung up. I stared out of the window. The moon, probably against its will, had moved off to one side of the sky, and would soon disappear behind a split level ranch house with a FOR SALE sign out front. An entire family could pick up and move, could change its life, I thought; then why the hell couldn't I?

That's when I saw my reflection in the window. As the moon departed, it left a fiesty, much more vocal replacement in its stead.

"Moron," it said to me. "You would even *consider* not taking them up on their offer?"

"But it's so complicated."

"What's so complicated? You go from point *a*, where there is nothing, to point *b*, where there may be everything. Point *b* is at least full of all-new things, and you would be shacking up with two beautiful men whose bodies you'd have access to whenever you wanted them. What could be less complicated than that?"

"Just what would I do in Chicago?"

"Survive. Explore. Enjoy. Fuck."

"You would consider that."

"And why shouldn't I? Someone's got to. By the way, congrats on jumping Garrick without my assistance. Maybe you're learning after all."

"Quiet," I hissed. "He'll hear you."

"I'll hear what?" Garrick had walked up sleepily behind me, rubbing his eyes and yawning. "Who are you talking to?"

"I'm just thinking out loud."

"About what?"

"I'm confused. I'm afraid. I'm at a crossroads." I sounded much too dramatic even to my own ears, and my reflection cringed, but that didn't stop me from going on in the same vein. "I read a book once where the main character had this pounding inside him, a voice really, a voice that was always crying out, 'I want, I want.' I have that voice too. A little more sibilant, perhaps, but it's there all the same. I hear it all the time. 'I want, I want.' I want so many things but I don't know how to get them. Hell, I don't even know what half of them are. Ah, but Garrick, I *want*."

He seemed slightly frightened by my speech. I hastened to tell him about my telephone conversation with Jamie and the plans for me that he and Mick had made.

"You think you'll do it?" Garrick asked.

"I don't know. I just don't know. What would you do?"

"Exactly what I've decided I'm going to do." He stood a little straighter and threw his chest out just a bit; he had an announcement. "I've made another decision. I'm not waiting until the end of the year to quit, and I'm not going to let Greg fire me come Monday morning. I'm leaving. I'm quitting. I don't want to be a teacher. It was all a mistake. When Greg unlocks that door Monday, I'm going to have my letter of resignation ready for him. I want out of here. I deserve better. I'm going home."

He waited, quite rightly, for my response. I gave him none. Instead, I pushed past him to stare out the window. "Who's that?" I asked.

"Who's who?"

I pointed out the window. In the distance, at the edge of the parking lot, just before everything dissolved in darkness, was a figure, a person. Garrick said he didn't see anything. I practically pressed his face through the glass trying to get him to focus on the right spot. When the figure took a few steps toward the building, I knew exactly who it was. He moved as if pushing the very night away from him. I quickly grabbed my clothing, still strewn around the office.

"Hurry," I said. "Get dressed. It's him."

"Him who?"

"Mick."

I flashed the office lights three times in order to attract Mick's attention. After much hesitancy, and three more flashes, he moved tentatively toward the building. When I thought he was within hearing distance, I leaned my head as far out of the window as I could and hissed his name. He looked around, then whispered, "Harper? Is that you? Where are you?

My continued hissing directed him to the window where half my head awaited him.

"What are you doing here this time of night?" he asked.

"We're thinking of redecorating the office as a surprise birthday present for our principal. We thought we'd better get some measurements."

"We?"

"Garrick, quit cowering in the shadows and come here a second, please. I want you to meet Mick Michaels."

They shook hands through the window. "I want to talk to you about something important, Harper," Mick said.

"Garrick," I asked, "Could you cower over there just a little longer?"

When Garrick had retreated, Mick requested that I come outside and talk, that what he had to say was too important to exchange through a pane of glass. I explained to him that we were trapped and that if he didn't mind, would he please enter the building the way Garrick and I had and see what he could do about freeing us. He thought about it for a moment. "Let's talk first," he said.

"But you said you didn't want to talk through a pane of glass."

"I changed my mind."

"Why don't we just wait to talk until you get us out of here?"

Mick's features screwed up unpleasantly in what was, I guessed, the first look of anger he had ever shown me. "Let's talk first," he said again, this time somewhat heatedly.

"What about?"

"Two things. First of all, I'm real sorry about you walking

in on that Douglas guy and me. It wasn't the best welcome to Chicago I could have given you. I didn't expect you until next weekend. Douglas means absolutely nothing to me. He just happened. I met him, and, well, you saw the results. I probably will never see him again. I really am sorry."

"You don't have to explain about Douglas. You don't have to explain about anything. I am certainly not illogical enough to think you're supposed to give up sex just because you and I like one another. I surely haven't given it up. However, I am just illogical enough to get my feelings hurt when I saw you two together."

"That isn't illogical. I don't know if you'll understand, but I'm almost glad you feel that way. It shows you care about me. So who have you been sleeping with anyway?"

"Let's stay on the subject, shall we?"

"So you're not mad at me about Douglas?"

"No."

"And you forgive me for hurting your feelings?"

"Yes."

"And you really can't get out of that office?"

"No."

"Then lean down here and kiss me."

I did as I was told, nearly wrenching my neck in the process. Retrieving my lips, I told him I already knew what the second thing was he wanted to talk about.

"You do?"

"Didn't Jamie tell you?"

"Tell me what?"

I explained that I assumed when Jamie told Mick to come rescue us from the school, he'd also told him that we'd had a lengthy telephone conversation about their plans for me.

"But Jamie didn't tell me to come to the school. That kid did."

"What kid?"

"The one at your apartment. The blond. He was wearing your bathrobe when he answered the door. He told me you were probably here. Who is he?"

"A nephew."

"Cute."

"However," I said firmly, steering the conversation away from Dean, "I do know what else you want to talk to me about. You want me to move to Chicago."

"And? What do you think?"

"I don't know what to think."

"But you're not coming to live with me, right?"

"I didn't say that."

"What are you saying?"

He was angry again. We stared at one another through the window. "Harper," he said at last. "This is the only chance I'm going to give you. Do you hear me? If you don't take this chance, if you don't take your life in your own hands and do something to improve your lot, then I don't want to have anything to do with you. If you don't say yes, Mick, I'm coming to Chicago, then this is the last time we'll be seeing each other."

It was my turn to be angry. "Just who in the hell do you think you are?" I demanded. Behind me I could hear Garrick rustle uncomfortably. "Who are you to tell me that my whole life has been nothing, that I'm a flop? Who are you to come around giving me ultimatums about uprooting everything I have in order to come live in a new city with two strangers? Just who in the hell do you think you are?" I thought I'd repeat *that* one for good measure.

Not matching my ire, Mick said almost sadly, "I think I'm someone who may very well be in love with you."

"You don't even know me," I answered. Then I laughed. "Perhaps that's the reason you can think you love me. Oh, I don't know, Mick. Get us out of here and we can go talk this over. There are so many details to be worked out."

"No. We can talk details for years and you'd still be here wasting yourself."

"Please let us out so we can talk."

"No. I'm not letting you out until you agree to move to Chicago."

"What?"

"Unless you say that you'll do as Jamie and I want, unless you say that on Monday morning you'll give notice, unless you promise to move to Chicago within a month, I'm going to leave you in that office. And, if I leave you in that office, you know what is going to happen to you Monday when they find you huddling all cramped on the floor. They're going to fire your ass, and then what will you do? You'll *have* to come to Chicago, but by then I won't want you. I mean it, if you say no now, we're through, even before it really begins. And I think you'd be tossing away something very special. So what's your answer, Harper? I hope you're susceptible to blackmail."

From behind me, Garrick said my name with a message in its pronunciation I could not interpret. My reflection made threatening gestures that were easily interpreted. What choice did I really have when it came right down to it? I did feel something potent for Mick, and certainly something very potent about my current lot in life. But change loomed before me like an ominous body of uncharted water. With a slight shiver, I mentally held my nose and plunged in. "All right," I said quietly. "I'll move to Chicago. Do what you and Jamie want. I'll quit on Monday and I'll be up there within the month."

"Perfect! Fantastic!" Mick cried as Garrick squeezed a shoulder from behind. "Lean down here and kiss me again." Puckered lips pressed near the pane.

"First get us out of here," I answered. "And in case you're interested, Mick Michaels, and you had better be, that's the last ultimatum you're ever going to give me."

"Oh, Harper, we're going to have so much fun together."

"Uh-huh."

I gave him directions to the English hall where, hopefully, the door by which we had entered was still unlocked. Then I told him how to find the Administrative Suite. After that, he was on his own; I said I hoped he knew how to pick locks. Garrick and I were quiet as we waited. Decisions had been made: we were both leaving. In the last few moments before our lives changed and our plans were set into action, we stood in the middle of Greg Prynne's office and held one another.

Mick took no time at all in negotiating the halls. Our release was not difficult either, in fact, it was embarrassingly easy, for a key had not actually been used on the door, but merely a latch. By turning it from vertical to horizontal, Mick freed us. "Now about that kiss?" he asked.

"But I don't even know you," Garrick said.

"I think he means me." I went into Mick's arms, but not before warning Garrick that if he touched Mick, I'd pull his hair. In Mick's grasp, so strong and certain somehow, I felt as if his plans for me were, in fact, for the best.

We retraced our steps through the school, and were about to emerge into the night, when I had a sudden desire to visit my classroom. I told Mick and Garrick to wait in the car, that I'd be there in no more than ten minutes. They protested, but I got my way. Even my reflection went with them, for I saw no more of him that night.

Light from a street lamp wafted through the windows of my room, polishing my desk, leaving a trail of white, like shining footsteps, across the blackboard. I walked all around the room, sitting in several chairs along the way, imagining what I looked like to students as I taught. I avoided sitting in Dean's seat. "So this is your realm," I said aloud, "Such as it is. Not much when you come to think of it."

I sat on my desk in the splotches of light and tried to

breathe normally; I was mostly unsuccessful. It was if an escape hatch had been thrown open somewhere and all the oxygen were rushing out of the room. Five minutes passed before I even moved. At last I jumped to my feet, bounding around the room in confused agitation. No one should be forced to make a decision so quickly, but I had made mine and I would stick to it. I grabbed the globe at the back of the room, and I destroyed the world. Bulletin boards I'd struggled hours to create came down in tatters, tacks falling like hail around me. I was about to sweep a shelf full of books to the floor when I stopped, suddenly calm, suddenly certain. I looked around the room again., After six years I was leaving it. I was a free man; the doors of the world were opening to me. To cry would have wasted time — I made a mental note to do it later — and I had no time to waste. I went to the blackboard. The sound of white chalk clicking and sliding against smooth slate filled the room, time impatiently tapping its foot awaiting my final departure. "I'm going away," I wrote very carefully in my best blackboard hand. The words shimmered in the streetlight. I wrote it again— "I'm going away" — saying it aloud for good measure. I was nearly out the door when I returned to the board and, hand shaking with anticipation, added a hasty but heartfelt, "Bye, bye."

Other books of interest from Alyson Publications

Don't miss our *free* book offer on the coupon at the end of this section.

☐ **ONE TEENAGER IN TEN: Writings by gay and lesbian youth,** edited by Ann Heron, $4.00. One teenager in ten is gay; here, twenty-six young people tell their stories: of coming to terms with being different, of the decision how — and whether — to tell friends and parents, and what the consequences were.

☐ **SWEET DREAMS,** by John Preston, $5.00. Who says heroes can't be gay? Not John Preston. In his new Alex Kane series, he has created a gay alternative to The Destroyer and The Executioner — a crusader against homophobia, whose only weakness is other men.

☐ **KINDRED SPIRITS,** edited by Jeffrey M. Elliot, $7.00. Science fiction offers an almost unlimited opportunity for writers to explore alternative ways of living; in these twelve stories, the reader has a chance to see twelve very different visions of what it could mean to be gay or lesbian in other worlds and other times.

☐ **THE TWO OF US,** by Larry Uhrig, $7.00. The author draws on his years of counseling with gay people to give some down-to-earth advice about what makes a relationship work. He gives special emphasis to the religious aspects of gay unions.

☐ **BETWEEN FRIENDS,** by Gillian E. Hanscombe, $7.00. Frances and Meg were friends in school years ago; now Frances is a married housewife while Meg is a lesbian involved in progressive politics. Through letters written between these women and their friends, the author weaves an engrossing story while exploring many vital lesbian and feminist issues.

☐ **THE ALEXANDROS EXPEDITION,** by Patricia Sitkin, $6.00. When Evan Talbot leaves on a mission to rescue an old schoolmate who has been imprisoned by fanatics in the Middle East, he doesn't realize that the trip will also involve his own coming out and the discovery of who it is that he really loves.

☐ **THE MOVIE LOVER,** by Richard Friedel, $7.00. The entertaining coming-out story of Burton Raider, who is so elegant that as a child he reads *Vogue* in his playpen. "The writing is fresh and crisp, the humor often hilarious," writes the *L.A. Times*.

☐ **CHINA HOUSE,** by Vincent Lardo, $5.00. This gay gothic romance/mystery has everything: two handsome lovers, a mysterious house on the hill, sounds in the night, and a father-son relationship that's closer than most.

☐ **DANNY,** by Margaret Sturgis, $7.00. High school teacher Tom York has a problem when the school board wants to censor many of the books he feels are most important for his classes to read. But all that pales in the face of the new difficulties that arise when he finds himself in an intense love affair with Danny, his most promising student.

☐ **DEATH TRICK,** by Richard Stevenson, $6.00. Meet Don Strachey, a private eye in the classic tradition but with one difference: he's gay. Here, writes Nathan Aldyne (author of *Vermilion*), Stevenson has "written a novel that is always clever and always entertaining and at the same time politically correct — quite a feat."

☐ **QUATREFOIL,** by James Barr, $7.00. Originally published in 1950, this book marks a milestone in gay writing: it introduced two of the first non-stereotyped gay characters to appear in American fiction. This story of two naval officers who become lovers gave readers of the fifties a rare chance to counteract the negative imagery that surrounded them.

□ **REFLECTIONS OF A ROCK LOBSTER: A story about growing up gay,** by Aaron Fricke, $5.00. When Aaron Fricke took a male date to the senior prom, no one was surprised: he'd gone to court to be able to do so, and the case had made national news. Here Aaron tells his story, and shows what gay pride can mean in a small New England town.

□ **DECENT PASSIONS,** by Michael Denneny, $7.00. What does it mean to be in love? Do the joys outweigh the pains? Those are some of the questions explored here as Denneny talks separately with each member of three unconventional relationships — a gay male couple, a lesbian couple, and an interracial couple — about all the little things that make up a relationship.

□ **COMING OUT RIGHT, A handbook for the gay male,** by Wes Muchmore and William Hanson, $6.00. The first steps into the gay world — whether it's a first relationship, a first trip to a gay bar, or coming out at work — can be full of unknowns. This book will make it easier. Here is advice on all aspects of gay life for both the inexperienced and the experienced.

The Gay Person's Guide to Media Action

Lesbian and Gay Media Advocates

Get this book free!

When were you last outraged by prejudiced media coverage of gay people? Chances are it hasn't been long. *Talk Back!* tells how you, in surprisingly little time, can do something about it.

If you order at least three other books from us, you may request a FREE copy of this important book. (See order form on next page.)

To get these books:

Ask at your favorite bookstore for the books listed here. You may also order by mail. Just fill out the coupon below, or use your own paper if you prefer not to cut up this book.

GET A FREE BOOK! When you order any three books listed here at the regular price, you may request a *free* copy of *Talk Back!*

— — — — — — — — — — — — — — — — —

Enclosed is $_____ for the following books. (Add $1.00 postage when ordering just one book; if you order two or more, we'll pay the postage.)

_____

_____

_____

_____

_____

_____

☐ Send a free copy of *Talk Back!* as offered above. I have ordered at least three other books.

name: _____

address: _____

city: _____ state: _____ zip: _____

ALYSON PUBLICATIONS
Dept. B-70, PO Box 2783, Boston, Mass. 02208

This offer expires June 30, 1987. After that date, please write for current catalog.